The NEWBERY CLASSICS
Dedicated to the memory of John Newbery
Printer for Children 1713 to 1767

CHILDREN'S STORIES
from DICKENS

Re-told by his Grand-daughter
MARY ANGELA DICKENS
and others

Illustrated by
HAROLD COPPING

DAVID McKAY COMPANY
604-608 South Washington Square, Philadelphia

CONTENTS

ILLUSTRATIONS

CHILDREN'S STORIES FROM DICKENS

THE RUNAWAY COUPLE

SUPPOSING a young gentleman not eight years old was to run away with a fine young woman of seven, would you consider that a queer start? That there is a start as I—the Boots at the Holly-Tree Inn—have seen with my own eyes; and I cleaned the shoes they ran away in, and they was so little that I couldn't get my hand into 'em.

"Master Harry Walmers's father, he lived at the Elms, away by Shooter's Hill, six or seven miles from London. He was uncommonly proud of Master Harry, as was his only child; but he didn't spoil him neither. He was a gentleman that had a will of his own, and an eye of his own, and that would be minded. Consequently, though he made quite a companion of the fine bright boy, still he kept the command over him, and the child *was* a child. I was under-gardener there at that time; and one morning Master Harry, he comes to me and says—

" 'Cobbs, how should you spell Norah, if you were asked?' and he took his little knife and began cutting that name in print all over the fence. The next day as it might be, he stops, along with Miss Norah, where I was hoeing weeds in the gravel, and says, speaking up—

" 'Cobbs, I like you! Why do I like you, do you think, Cobbs? Because Norah likes you.'

" 'Indeed, sir,' says I. 'That's very gratifying.'

" 'Gratifying, Cobbs?' says Master Harry. 'It's better than a million of the brightest diamonds, to be liked by Norah. You're going away, ain't you, Cobbs? Then you shall be our head gardener when we're married.' And he tucks her, in her little sky-blue mantle, under his arm, and walks away.

"I was the Boots at this identical Holly Tree Inn when one summer afternoon the coach drives up, and out of the coach gets these two children. The young gentleman gets out; hands his lady out; gives the guard something for himself; says to my governor, the landlord: 'We're to stop here to-night, please. Sitting-room and two bedrooms will be required. Mutton chops and cherry pudding for two!' and tucks her under his arm, and walks into the house, much bolder than brass.

"I had seen 'em without their seeing me, and I give the governor my views of the expedition they was upon. 'Cobbs,' says my governor, 'if this is so, I must set off myself and quiet their friends' minds.   In which case you must keep your eye upon 'em, and humor 'em, until I come back.   But before I take these measures, Cobbs, I should wish you to find out from themselves whether your opinion is correct.'

"So I goes upstairs, and there I finds Master Harry on an e-normous sofa a-drying the eyes of Miss Norah with his pocket handkercher. Their little legs was entirely off the ground, of course, and it really is not possible to express how small them children looked. 'It's Cobbs!   It's Cobbs!' cries Master Harry, and he comes a-running to me, and catching hold of my hand.   Miss Norah, she comes running to me on t'other side, and catching hold of my t'other hand, and they both jump for joy. And what I had took to be the case was the case.

" 'We're going to be married, Cobbs, at Gretna Green,' says the boy.   'We've run away on purpose.   Norah has been in rather low spirits, Cobbs; but she'll be happy now we have found you to be our friend.'

"I give you my word and honor upon it that, by way of luggage the lady had got a parasol, a smelling-bottle, a round and a half of cold buttered toast, eight peppermint drops, and a doll's hair-brush. The gentleman had got about a dozen yards of string, a knife, three or four sheets of writing-paper folded up surprisingly small, a orange, and a chaney mug with his name on it.

" 'What may be the exact nature of your plans, sir?' says I.

" 'To go on,' replies the boy, 'in the morning, and be married to-morrow.'

" 'Just so, sir. Well, sir, if you will excuse my having the freedom to give an opinion, vhat I should recommend would be this. I'm acquainted with a pony, sir, which would take you and Mrs. Harry Walmers junior to the end of your journey in a very short space of time.

I am not altogether sure, sir, that the pony will be at liberty to-morrow, but even if you had to wait for him it might be worth your while.'

"They clapped their hands and jumped for joy, and called me 'Good Cobbs!' and 'Dear Cobbs!' and says I, 'Is there anything you want at present, sir?'

" 'We should like some cakes after dinner,' answers Mr. Harry, 'and two apples—and jam. With dinner we should like to have toast and water. But Norah has always been accustomed to half a glass of currant wine at dessert, and so have I.'

" 'They shall be ordered, sir,' I answered, and away I went; and the way in which all the women in the house went on about that boy and his bold spirit was a thing to see. They climbed up all sorts of places to get a look at him, and they peeped, seven deep, through the keyhole.

"In the evening, after the governor had set off for the Elms, I went into the room to see how the runaway couple was getting on. The gentleman was on the window seat, supporting the lady in his arms. She had tears upon her face, and was lying very tired and half asleep, with her head upon his shoulder.

" 'Mrs. Harry Walmers junior fatigued, sir?'

" 'Yes, she's tired, Cobbs; she's been in low spirits again; she isn't used to being in a strange place, you see. Could you bring a Norfolk biffin, Cobbs? I think that would do her good.'

"Well, I fetched the biffin, and Master Harry fed her with a spoon; but the lady being heavy with sleep and rather cross, I suggested bed, and called a chambermaid, but Master Harry must needs escort her himself, and carry the candle for her. After embracing her at her own door he retired to his room, where I softly locked him in.

"They consulted me at breakfast (they had ordered sweet milk and water, and toast and currant jelly, over night) about the pony, and I told 'em that it did unfortunately happen that the pony was half clipped, but that he'd be finished clipping in the course of the day, and that to-morrow morning at eight o'clock he would be ready. My own opinion is that Mrs. Harry Walmers junior was beginning to give in. She hadn't had her hair curled when she went to bed, and she didn't seem quite up to brushing it herself, and its getting into her eyes put her out. But nothing put out Mr. Harry. He sat behind his breakfast cup tearing away at the jelly, as if he'd been his own father.

"In the course of the morning, Master Harry rung the bell—it was surprising how that there boy did carry on—and said in a sprightly way, 'Cobbs, is there any good walks in the neighborhood?'

" 'Yes, sir, there's Love Lane.'

" 'Get out with you, Cobbs!'—that was that there mite's expression—'you're joking.'

" 'Begging your pardon, sir, there really is a Love Lane, and a pleasant walk it is; and proud shall I be to show it to yourself and Mrs. Harry Walmers junior.'

"Well, I took him down Love Lane to the water meadows, and there Master Harry would have drowned himself in another minute a-getting out a water lily for her. But they was tired out. All being so new and strange to them, they were as tired as tired could be. And they laid down on a bank of daisies and fell asleep.

"They woke up at last, and then one thing was getting pretty clear to me, namely, that Mrs. Harry Walmers junior's temper was on the move. When Master Harry took her

round the waist, she said he 'teased her so';
and when he says, 'Norah, my young May
moon, your Harry tease you?' she tells him,
'Yes, and I want to go home.'

"A boiled fowl, and baked bread and butter
pudding brought Mrs. Walmers up a little;
but I could have wished, I must privately own,
to have seen her more sensible to the voice of
love and less abandoning herself to the cur-
rants in the pudding. However, Master
Harry, he kep' up, and his noble heart was as
fond as ever. Mrs. Walmers turned very
sleepy about dusk, and began to cry. Therefore, Mrs. Walmers went off to bed as per
yesterday; and Master Harry ditto repeated.

"About eleven at night comes back the governor in a chaise, along of Master Harry's
father and a elderly lady. And Master
Harry's door being unlocked by me, Master
Harry's father goes in, goes up to the bedside,
bends gently down, and kisses the little sleep-

ing face.   Then he stands looking at it for a moment, looking wonderfully like it; and then he gently shakes the little shoulder.   'Harry, my dear boy! Harry!'

"Master Harry starts up and looks at his pa.   Such is the honor of that mite, that he looks at me, too, to see whether he has brought me into trouble.

" 'I am not angry, my child.   I only want you to dress yourself and come home.'

" 'Yes, pa.'   Master Harry dresses himself quick.

" 'Please may I—please, dear pa—may I —kiss Norah before I go?'

"Master Harry's father he takes Master Harry in his hand, and I leads the way with the candle to that other bedroom where the elderly lady is seated by the bed, and poor little Mrs. Harry Walmers junior is fast asleep.   There the father lifts the boy up to the pillow, and he lays his little face down for an instant by the little warm face of poor little Mrs. Harry Walmers junior, and gently draws it to him.

"And that's all about it.   Master Harry's father drove away in the chaise having hold of Master Harry's hand.   The elderly lady and Mrs. Harry Walmers junior that was never to be (she married a captain long after and went to India) went off next day."

OLIVER TWIST

ONCE upon a time there was born in a country workhouse a baby boy. He was a poor, weakly little child, and at the time of his birth his mother died, and nobody knew who she was, and nobody had heard of his father or any of his relations, so he was just a poor little atom in this wide, wide world of ours.

The workhouse people called him Oliver Twist, and brought him up with a lot of other miserable children who were also without fathers or mothers. The poor boy was beaten and half-starved, and was altogether as unhappy as unhappy can be, for workhouses were different in those days to what they are now.

The room in which the boys were fed was a

large stone hall, with a copper at one end, out of which the master, dressed in an apron for the purpose, and assisted by one or two women, ladled the gruel at meal-times. Of this festive composition each boy had one porringer, and no more—except on occasions of great public rejoicing, when he had two ounces and a quarter of bread besides. The bowls never wanted washing. The boys polished them with their spoons till they shone again; and, when they had performed this operation (which never took very long, the spoons being nearly as large as the bowls), they would sit staring at the copper with such eager eyes as if they could have devoured the very bricks of which it was composed, employing themselves meanwhile in sucking their fingers most assiduously, with the view of catching up any stray splashes of gruel that might have been cast thereon. Boys have generally excellent appetites. Oliver Twist and his companions suffered the tortures of slow starvation for several months; at last they got so voracious and wild with hunger that one boy, who was tall for his age, and hadn't been used to that sort of thing (for his father had kept a small cook-shop), hinted darkly to his companions that unless he had another basin of gruel *per diem* he was afraid he might some night happen to eat the boy who slept next him, who happened to be a weakly youth of tender age. He had a wild, hungry eye, and they implicitly believed him.   A council was held; lots were cast who should walk up to the master after supper that evening, and ask for more, and it fell to Oliver Twist.

The evening arrived.   The boys took their places.   The master, in his cook's uniform, stationed himself at the copper, his pauper assistants ranged themselves behind him, the gruel was served out, and a long grace was said over the short commons.   The gruel disappeared. The boys whispered to each other and winked at Oliver, while his next neighbors nudged him. Child as he was, he was desperate with hunger and reckless with misery. He rose from the table, and advancing to the master, basin and spoon in hand, said, somewhat alarmed at his own temerity:

"Please, sir, I want some more."

The master was a fat healthy man; but he turned very pale. He gazed in stupefied astonishment on the small rebel for some seconds, and then clung for support to the copper. The assistants were paralyzed with wonder, the boys with fear.

"What!" said the master at length, in a faint voice.

"Please, sir," replied Oliver, "I want some more."

The master aimed a blow at Oliver's head with the ladle, pinioned him in his arms, and shrieked aloud for the beadle.

The board was sitting in solemn conclave, when Mr. Bumble, the Beadle, rushed into the room in great excitement, and addressing the gentleman in the high chair, said:

"Mr. Limbkins, I beg your pardon, sir! Oliver Twist has asked for more!"

There was a general start. Horror was depicted on every countenance.

"For *more!*" said Mr. Limbkins. "Compose yourself, Bumble, and answer me distinctly. Do I understand that he asked for more after he had eaten the supper allotted by the dietary?"

"He did, sir," replied Bumble.

"That boy will be hung," said a gentleman in a white waistcoat. "I know that boy will be hung."

Nobody controverted the prophetic gentleman's opinion. An animated discussion took place. Oliver was ordered into instant confinement, and a bill was next morning pasted

on the outside of the gate offering a reward
of five pounds to anybody who would take
Oliver Twist off the hands of the parish. In
other words, five pounds and Oliver Twist
were offered to any man or woman who wanted
an apprentice to any trade, business or calling.

Well, the bill on the gate had its effect, and
Oliver, at the early age of ten, left the workhouse to earn his living. He was apprenticed
to an undertaker called Mr. Sowerberry, and
here he was as badly treated as he had been
at the workhouse. Mr. Sowerberry had another apprentice, named Noah Claypole, who
was a horrid, disagreeable boy. He and the
servant Charlotte were continually bullying
poor little Oliver.

One day Noah went too far; he abused
Oliver's mother.

"Work'us," said Noah—he always called
Oliver "Work'us"—"how's your mother?"

"She's dead," replied Oliver. "Don't you say anything about her to me!"

Oliver's color rose as he said this, he breathed quickly, and there was a curious working of the mouth and nostrils, which Mr. Claypole thought must be the immediate precursor of a violent fit of crying. Under this impression he returned to the charge.

"What did she die of, Work'us?" said Noah.

"Of a broken heart some of our old nurses told me," replied Oliver, more as if he were talking to himself than answering Noah. "I think I know what it must be to die of that!"

"Tol de rol lol lol, right fol lairy, Work'us," said Noah, as a tear rolled down Oliver's cheek. "What's set you a-snivelling now?"

"Not *you*," replied Oliver, hastily brushing the tear away. "Don't think it."

"Oh, not me, eh?" sneered Noah.

"No, not you," replied Oliver sharply. "There, that's enough. Don't say anything more to me about her; you'd better not!"

"Better not!" exclaimed Noah. "Well! Better not! Work'us, don't be impudent. *Your* mother, too! She was a nice 'un, she was. Oh, Lor!" And here Noah nodded his head expressively, and curled up as much of his small red nose as muscular action could collect together for the occasion.

"Yer know, Work'us," continued Noah, emboldened by Oliver's silence, and speaking in a jeering tone of affected pity—of all tones the most annoying—"yer know, Work'us, it can't be helped now, and of course yer couldn't help it then, and I'm very sorry for it, and I'm sure we all are, and pity yer very much. But yer must know, Work'us, yer mother was a regular right-down bad 'un."

"What did you say?" inquired Oliver, looking up very quickly.

"A right-down bad 'un, Work'us," replied Noah, coolly. "And it's a great deal better, Work'us, that she died when she did, or else she'd have been hard laboring in Bridewell, or transported, or hung, which is more likely than either, isn't it?"

Crimson with fury, Oliver started up, overthrew the chair and table, seized Noah by the throat, shook him in the violence of his rage till his teeth chattered in his head, and, collecting his whole force into one heavy blow, felled him to the ground.

A minute ago the boy had looked the quiet, mild, dejected creature that harsh treatment had made him. But his spirit was roused at last; the cruel insult to his dead mother had set his blood on fire. His breast heaved; his attitude was erect; his eye bright and vivid; his whole person changed, as he stood glaring over the cowardly tormentor who now lay crouching at his feet, and defied him with an energy he had never known before.

"He'll murder me!" blubbered Noah. "Charlotte! Missis! Here's the new boy a-murdering of me! Help! help! Oliver's gone mad! Charlotte!"

Noah's shouts were responded to by a loud scream from Charlotte and a louder from Mrs. Sowerberry, the former of whom rushed into the kitchen by a side-door, while the latter paused on the staircase till she was quite certain that it was consistent with the preservation of human life to come further down.

"Oh, you little wretch!" screamed Charlotte, seizing Oliver with her utmost force, which was about equal to that of a moderately strong man in particularly good training. "Oh, you little un-grate-ful, mur-de-rous, horrid villain!" And between every syllable Charlott gave Oliver a blow with all her might, accompanying it with a scream for the benefit of society.

Charlotte's fist was by no means a light one; but, lest it should not be effectual in calming Oliver's wrath, Mrs. Sowerberry plunged into the kitchen and assisted to hold him with one hand while she scratched his face with the other. In this favorable position of affairs Noah rose from the ground and pommelled him behind.

This was rather too violent exercise to last long. When they were all three wearied out and could tear and beat no longer, they dragged Oliver, struggling and shouting, but nothing daunted, into the dust-cellar, and there locked him up. This being done, Mrs. Sowerberry sank into a chair and burst into tears.

"Bless her, she's going off!" said Charlotte. "A glass of water, Noah, dear. Make haste!"

"Oh! Charlotte," said Mrs. Sowerberry, speaking as well as she could through a deficiency of breath and a sufficiency of cold water, which Noah had poured over her head and shoulders. "Oh! Charlotte, what a mercy we have not all been murdered in our beds!"

"Ah! mercy indeed, ma'am," was the reply. "I only hope this'll teach master not to have any more of these dreadful creatures that are born to be murderers and robbers from their very cradle. Poor Noah! He was all but killed, ma'am, when I come in."

"Poor fellow!" said Mrs. Sowerberry, looking pityingly on the charity-boy.

Noah, whose top waistcoat-button might have been somewhere on a level with the crown of Oliver's head, rubbed his eyes with the inside of his wrists while this commiseration was bestowed upon him, and performed some affecting tears and sniffs.

"What's to be done?" exclaimed Mrs. Sowerberry. "Your master's not at home, there's not a man in the house, and he'll kick that

door down in ten minutes." Oliver's vigor-
ous plunges against the bit of timber in question rendered this occurrence highly probable.

"Dear, dear! I don't know, ma'am," said
Charlotte, "unless we send for the police of-
ficers."

"Or the millingtary," suggested Mr. Claypole.

"No, no," said Mrs. Sowerberry, bethink-
ing herself of the Beadle. "Run to Mr.
Bumble, Noah, and tell him to come here directly, and not to lose a minute; never mind
your cap! Make haste! You can hold a
knife to that black eye as you run along. It'll
keep the swelling down."

Noah did not stop to reply, but started off
at his fullest speed; and very much it astonished the people who were out walking to see
a charity-boy tearing through the streets pell-
mell, with no cap on his head and a clasp-knife
at his eye.

Poor Oliver was terribly punished for this, so much so that he determined to run away; but it was not until he was left alone in the silence and stillness of the gloomy workshop of the undertaker that Oliver gave way to the feelings which the day's treatment may be supposed likely to have awakened in a mere child.   He had listened to their taunts with a look of contempt; he had borne the lash without a cry, for he felt that pride swelling in his heart which would have kept down a shriek to the last, though they had roasted him alive.   But now, when there was none to see or hear him, he fell upon his knees on the floor, and, hiding his face in his hands, wept such tears as, God send for the credit of our nature, few so young may ever have cause to pour out before Him!

For a long time Oliver remained motionless in this attitude.   The candle was burning low in the socket when he rose to his feet.

Having gazed cautiously round him and listened intently, he gently undid the fastenings of the door and looked abroad.

It was a cold, dark night. The stars seemed to the boy's eyes farther from the earth than he had ever seen them before; there was no wind, and the somber shadows thrown by the trees upon the ground looked sepulchral and deathlike from being so still. He softly reclosed the door. Having availed himself of the expiring light of the candle to tie up in a handkerchief the few articles of wearing apparel he had, he sat himself down upon a bench to wait for morning.

With the first ray of light that struggled through the crevices in the shutters Oliver arose, and again unbarred the door. One timid look around, one moment's pause of hesitation; he had closed it behind him, and was in the open street.

He looked to the right and to the left, uncertain whither to fly. He remembered to have seen the wagons as they went out toiling up the hill. He took the same route, and, arriving at a footpath across the fields, which he knew, after some distance, led out again into the road, struck into it, and walked quickly on.

Along this same footpath Oliver well remembered he had trotted beside Mr. Bumble, the Beadle. His heart beat quickly when he bethought himself of this, and he half resolved to turn back. He had come a long way, though, and should lose a great deal of time by doing so. Besides, it was so early that there was very little fear of his being seen, so he walked on.

He reached a house. There was no appearance of its inmates stirring at that early hour. Oliver stopped and peeped into the garden. A child was weeding one of the little beds; as he stopped, he raised his pale face

Mr. Bumble and Oliver Twist.   (*Page 36*)

and disclosed the features of one of his former
companions. Oliver felt glad to see him before he went, for, though younger than himself, he had been his little friend and playmate.
They had been beaten and starved and shut
up together many and many a time.

"Hush, Dick!" said Oliver, as the boy ran
to the gate and thrust his thin arm between
the rails to greet him. "Is any one up?"

"Nobody but me," replied the child.

"You mustn't say you saw me, Dick," said
Oliver. "I am running away. They beat
and ill-use me, Dick, and I am going to seek
my fortune some long way off. I don't know
where. How pale you are!"

"I heard the doctor tell them I was dying,"
replied the child with a faint smile. "I am
very glad to see you, dear; but don't stop,
don't stop!"

"Yes, yes, I will, to say good-bye to you,"
replied Oliver. "I shall see you again, Dick.

I know I shall! You will be well and happy!"

"I hope so," replied the child. "After I am dead, but not before. I know the doctor must be right, Oliver, because I dream so much of heaven and angels and kind faces that I never see when I am awake. Kiss me," said the child, climbing up the low gate and flinging his little arms round Oliver's neck. "Good-by, dear! God bless you!"

The blessing was from a young child's lips, but it was the first that Oliver had ever heard invoked upon his head, and through the struggles and sufferings and troubles and changes of his after life he never once forgot it.

So this poor, friendless boy trudged off to London. He had no idea what he was going to do, where he was going to sleep, or when he would have his next meal; all he wanted was to get away from the cruel, unhappy life he had been leading.

Unfortunately, Oliver was to suffer worse miseries. For seven weary days he begged his way, sleeping under haystacks and such-like places, and was nearly dying of starvation and hunger when he met a strange boy. This boy, who was some years older than Oliver, gave him something to eat, and then took him to his home.

It was an awful home this, where the boy took Oliver, and awful people lived in it—horrible, wicked people, who lived entirely by stealing. Oliver was an innocent lad, and did not discover for some time that he was living with thieves; but one day he was out with the boy who had taken him home and another boy, when they saw an old gentleman standing by a bookstall. Immediately the two boys who were with Oliver walked stealthily across the road and slunk close behind the old gentleman. Oliver walked a few paces after them, and not knowing whether to advance or retire, stood looking on in silent amazement.

The old gentleman was a very respectable-looking personage, with a powdered head and gold spectacles. He was dressed in a bottle-green coat with a black velvet collar, wore white trousers, and carried a smart bamboo cane under his arm. He had taken up a book from the stall; and there he stood reading away as hard as if he were in his elbow-chair in his own study. It is very possible that he fancied himself there indeed, for it was plain, from his utter abstraction, that he saw not the bookstall, nor the street, nor the boys, nor, in short, anything but the book itself, which he was reading straight through, turning over the leaf when he got to the bottom of a page, beginning at the top line of the next one and going regularly on with the greatest interest and eagerness.

What was Oliver's horror and alarm, as he

stood a few paces off, looking on with his
eyelids as wide open as they would possibly
go, to see one of the boys plunge his hand into
the old gentleman's pocket, and draw from
thence a handkerchief! To see him hand
the same to the other boy, and finally to behold them both running away round the corner
at full speed!

Oliver stood for a moment with the blood
so tingling through all his veins from terror
that he felt as if he were in a burning fire,
then, confused and frightened, he took to his
heels, and not knowing what he did, made off
as fast as he could lay his feet to the ground.

This was all done in a minute's space. In
the very instant when Oliver began to run, the
old gentleman, putting his hand to his pocket
and missing his handkerchief, turned sharp
round. Seeing the boy scudding away at
such a rapid pace he very naturally concluded
him to be the depredator, and, shouting "Stop

thief!" with all his might, made off after him, book in hand.

But the old gentleman was not the only person who raised the hue and cry. The two young thieves, unwilling to attract public attention by running down the open street, had merely retired into the very first doorway round the corner. They no sooner heard the cry and saw Oliver running than, guessing exactly how the matter stood, they issued forth with great promptitude, and, shouting "Stop thief!" too, joined in the pursuit like good citizens.

Although Oliver had been brought up by philosophers he was not theoretically acquainted with the beautiful axiom that self-preservation is the first law of nature. If he had been, perhaps he would have been prepared for this. Not being prepared, however, it alarmed him the more; so away he went like the wind, with the old gentleman and the two boys roaring and shouting behind him.

"Stop thief! Stop thief!" There is a magic in the sound. The tradesman leaves his counter and the carman his wagon, the butcher throws down his tray, the baker his basket, the milkman his pail, the errand-boy his parcels, the school-boy his marbles, the pavior his pickaxe, the child his battledore. Away they run pell-mell, helter-skelter, slap-dash, tearing, yelling and screaming, knocking down the passengers as they turn the corners, rousing up the dogs and astonishing the fowls; and streets, squares and courts re-echo with the sound.

"Stop thief! Stop thief!" The cry is taken up by a hundred voices, and the crowd accumulates at every turning. Away they fly, splashing through the mud and rattling along the pavements; up go the windows, out

run the people, onward tears the mob, a whole
audience desert Punch in the very thickest of
the plot, and joining the rushing throng swell
the shout, and lend fresh vigor to the cry—

"Stop thief!   Stop thief!"

"Stop thief!   Stop thief!"   There is a
passion *for hunting something* deeply im-
planted in the human breast.   One wretched,
breathless child, panting with exhaustion, terror in his looks, agony in his eyes, large drops
of perspiration streaming down his face,
strains every nerve to make head upon his
pursuers, and as they follow on his track and
gain upon him every instant they hail his de-
creasing strength with still louder shouts, and
whoop and scream with joy, "Stop thief!"

Stopped at last!   A clever blow!   He is
down upon the pavement, and the crowd eagerly gather round him, each new-comer jos-
tling and struggling with the others to catch

a glimpse. "Stand aside!" "Give him a little air!" "Nonsense, he don't deserve it!" "Where's the gentleman?" "Here he is, coming down the street." "Make room there for the gentleman!" "Is this the boy, sir?" "Yes."

Oliver lay, covered with mud and dust, and bleeding from the mouth, looking wildly round upon the heap of faces that surrounded him, when the old gentleman was officiously dragged and pushed into the circle by the foremost of the pursuers.

"Yes," said the gentleman, "I am afraid it is the boy."

"Afraid!" murmured the crowd. "That's a good 'un."

"Poor fellow!" said the gentleman; "he has hurt himself."

"*I* did that, sir," said a great lubberly fellow, stepping forward; "and preciously *I* cut my knuckle agin' his mouth. *I* stopped him, sir."

The fellow touched his hat with a grin, expecting something for his pains; but the old gentleman, eyeing him with an expression of dislike, looked anxiously round as if he contemplated running away himself, which it is very possible he might have attempted to do, and thus afforded another chase, had not a police-officer (who is generally the last person to arrive in such cases) at that moment made his way through the crowd, and seized Oliver by the collar.

"Come, get up!" said the man roughly.

"It wasn't me, indeed, sir! Indeed, indeed, it was two other boys," said Oliver, clasping his hands passionately, and looking round. "They are here somewhere."

"Oh, no, they ain't," said the officer. He meant this to be ironical, but it was true besides, for the real thieves had filed off down the first convenient court they came to. "Come, get up!"

"Don't hurt him," said the old gentleman compassionately.

"Oh, no, I won't hurt him," replied the officer, tearing his jacket half off his back in proof thereof. "Come, I know you; it won't do. Will you stand upon your legs?"

Oliver, who could hardly stand, made a shift to raise himself on his feet, and was at once lugged along the streets by the jacket-collar at a rapid pace. The gentleman walked on with them by the officer's side, and as many of the crowd as could achieve the feat got a little ahead and stared back at Oliver from time to time. The boys shouted in triumph, and on they went.

Poor Oliver was taken before a magistrate, and was tried and sentenced to go to prison for three months; and the police were taking the boy away when an elderly man of decent but poor appearance, clad in an old suit of black, rushed hastily into the office, and advanced towards the magistrate.

"Stop! stop! Don't take him away! For heaven's sake, stop a moment!" cried the newcomer, breathless with haste.

"I saw three boys," continued the man, "two others and the prisoner here, loitering on the opposite side of the way when this gentleman was reading. The robbery was committed by another boy. I saw it done, and I saw that this boy was perfectly amazed and stupefied by it." Having by this time recovered a little breath, the worthy bookstall-keeper proceeded to relate, in a more coherent manner, the exact circumstances of the robbery.

So it happened that Oliver did not go to prison, but instead was taken home by the old gentleman who had been robbed, and was tenderly cared for. Indeed, Oliver was happy for the first time in his life.

It would be very nice to be able to tell you that Oliver stayed with this kind old gentleman; but, alas! it was not so. Those wicked thieves stole Oliver away, and took him back to their awful home, and threatened to kill him if he ran away again.

Among these thieves there was one more desperate and wicked than the others. His name was Bill Sikes. Well, one night Sikes and another man went out to rob a house, and took Oliver with them to help, poor boy!

When they came to the house, which was in the country, Sikes, who was in the garden, put Oliver gently through a little window, and told him to go and open the street door and let them in.

"Take this lantern," said Sikes. "You see the stairs afore you?"

Oliver, more dead than alive, gasped out, "Yes." Sikes, pointing to the street door with the pistol-barrel, briefly advised him to take notice that he was well within shot all the way, and that if he faltered he would fall dead that instant.

"It's done in a minute," said Sikes, in the same low whisper. "Directly I leave go of you do your work. Hark!"

"What's that?" whispered the other man. They listened intently.

"Nothing," said Sikes, releasing his hold of Oliver.

"Now!"

In the short time he had had to collect his senses the boy had firmly resolved that, whether he died in the attempt or not, he would make one effort to dart upstairs from the hall and alarm the family.

Filled with this idea he advanced at once, but stealthily.

"Come back!" suddenly cried Sikes aloud. "Back! back!"

Scared by the sudden breaking of the dead stillness of the place, and by a loud cry which followed it, Oliver let his lantern fall, and knew not whether to advance or fly.

The cry was repeated—a light appeared—a vision of two terrified half-dressed men at the top of the stairs swam before his eyes—a flash—a loud noise—a smoke—a crash somewhere, but where he knew not—and he staggered back.

Sikes muttered horribly to himself, grinding his teeth with rage, as he hurried along. Then for a moment he rested the body of the wounded boy across his bended knee, and turned his head for an instant to look back at his pursuers.

There was little to be made out in the mist and darkness; but the loud shouting of men vibrated through the air, and the barking of the neighboring dogs, roused by the sound of the alarm-bell, resounded in every direction.

"Stop, you hound!" cried the robber, shouting after the other burglar, Toby Crackit, who, making the best use of his long legs, was already ahead—"Stop!"

The repetition of the word brought Toby to a dead standstill, for he was not quite satisfied that he was beyond the range of pistol-shot, and Sikes was in no mood to be played with.

"Bear a hand with the boy," roared Sikes, beckoning furiously to his confederate. "Come back!"

Toby made a show of returning but ventured in a low voice, broken for want of breath to intimate considerable reluctance as he came slowly along.

"Quicker!" cried Sikes, laying the boy in a dry ditch at his feet, and drawing a pistol from his pocket. "Don't play the booby with me."

At this moment the noise grew louder, and Sikes again looking round could discern that the men who had given chase were already climbing the gate of the field in which he stood, and that a couple of dogs were some paces in advance of them.

"It's all up, Bill," cried Toby; "drop the kid and show 'em your heels."

With this parting advice Mr. Crackit, preferring the chance of being shot by his friend to the certainty of being taken by his enemies, fairly turned tail, and darted off at full speed.

Sikes clenched his teeth, took one look round, threw over the prostrate form of Oliver the cape in which he had been hurriedly muffled, ran along the front of the hedge as if to distract the attention of those behind from the spot where the boy lay, paused for a second before another hedge which met it at right angles, and whirling his pistol high into the air, cleared it at a bound, and was gone.

"Ho, ho, there!" cried a tremulous voice in the rear. "Pincher, Neptune, come here, come here!"

The dogs, which in common with their masters seemed to have no particular relish for the sport in which they were engaged, readily answered to this command, and three men, who had by this time advanced some distance into the field, stopped to take counsel together.

The result of their talk was that they returned to their home without finding poor Oliver. As a matter of fact, they were all very nervous, for it's by no means a pleasant thing to have to turn out of a warm bed on a cold night to hunt armed burglars—desperate, wicked men who would not hesitate to shoot you.

*   *   *   *   *

The air grew colder as day came slowly on, and the mist rolled along the ground like a

dense cloud of smoke; the grass was wet, the
pathways and low places were all mire and
water, and the damp breath of an unwhole-
some wind went languidly by with a hollow
moaning.　Still Oliver lay motionless and insensible on the spot where Sikes had left him.

Morning drew on apace; the air became
more sharp and piercing as its first dull hue—
the death of night rather than the birth of day
—glimmered faintly in the sky.　The objects
which had looked dim and terrible in the darkness grew more and more defined, and gradually resolved into their familiar shapes.
The rain came down thick and fast, and pat-
tered noisily among the leafless bushes.　But
Oliver felt it not as it beat against him, for he
still lay stretched, helpless and unconscious,
on his bed of clay.

At length a low cry of pain broke the stillness that prevailed, and, uttering it, the boy
awoke.　His left arm, rudely bandaged in a

shawl, hung heavy and useless at his side, and the bandage was saturated with blood.

He was so weak that he could scarcely raise himself into a sitting posture, and when he had done so, he looked feebly around for help, and groaned with pain.   Trembling in every joint from cold and exhaustion, he made an effort to stand upright, but shuddering from head to foot, fell prostrate on the ground.

After a short return of the stupor in which he had been so long plunged, Oliver, urged by a creeping sickness at his heart, which seemed to warn him that if he lay there he must surely die, got upon his feet and essayed to walk.

His head was dizzy, and he staggered to and fro like a drunken man; but he kept up nevertheless, and, with his head drooping languidly on his breast, went stumbling onward he knew not whither.

And now hosts of bewildering and confused

ideas came crowding on his mind. He
seemed to be still walking between Sikes and
Crackit, who were angrily disputing, for the
very words they said sounded in his ears; and
when he caught his own attention, as it were,
by making some violent effort to save himself
from falling, he found that he was talking to
them.

Then he was alone with Sikes, plodding on
as they had done the previous day and as
shadowy people passed them by, he felt the
robber's grasp upon his wrist. Suddenly he
started back at the report of firearms, and
there rose into the air loud cries and shouts;
lights gleamed before his eyes, and all was
noise and tumult as some unseen hand bore
him hurriedly away. Through all these rapid
visions there ran an undefined, uneasy con-
sciousness of pain, which wearied and tormented him incessantly.

Thus he staggered on, creeping almost

mechanically between the bars of gates or through hedge-gaps as they came in his way, until he reached a road; and here the rain began to fall so heavily that it roused him.

He looked about, and saw that at no great distance there was a house, which perhaps he could reach. Seeing his condition they might have compassion on him, and if they did not it would be better, he thought, to die near human beings than in the lonely open fields.

He summoned up all his strength for one last trial, and bent his faltering steps towards it.

As he drew nearer to this house a feeling came over him that he had seen it before. He remembered nothing of its details, but the shape and aspect of the building seemed familiar to him.

That garden wall! On the grass inside he had fallen on his knees last night and prayed

the two men's mercy. It was the very same
house they had attempted to rob. Oliver felt
such fear come over him when he recognized
the place, that for the instant, he forgot the
agony of his wound, and thought only of
flight!

Flight! He could scarcely stand; and if
he were in full possession of all the best powers of his slight and youthful frame, where
could he fly to? He pushed against the
garden-gate; it was unlocked, and swung open
on its hinges.

He tottered across the lawn, climbed the
steps, knocked faintly at the door, and his
whole strength failing him, sank down against
one of the pillars of the little portico.

     *   *   *   *   *

And now what happened to this poor
wretched little boy? The door was opened,
and he was recognized as one of the daring

burglars.   He was seized and dragged into the house by the man-servant, and a doctor was sent for.

Doctor Losberne was one of the kindest men in the world, and he had Oliver put to bed, and dressed his wound and did everything he could for him.   Then afterwards he saw Mrs. Maylie, the lady of the house, and her daughter Rose, to tell them about the dreadful burglar that had broken into the house the night before.

"This is a very extraordinary thing, Mrs. Maylie," said the doctor, standing with his back to the door as if to keep it shut.

"He is not in danger, I hope?" said the old lady.

"Why, that would not be an extraordinary thing, under the circumstances," replied the doctor, "though I don't think he is.   Have you seen this thief?"

"No," rejoined the old lady.

"Nor heard anything about him?"

"No. Rose wished to see the man," said Mrs. Maylie, "but I wouldn't hear of it."

"Humph!" rejoined the doctor. "There's nothing very• alarming in his appearance. Have you any objection to see him in my presence?"

"If it be necessary," replied the old lady, "certainly not."

"Then I think it is necessary," said the doctor; "at all events, I am quite sure that you would deeply regret not having done so if you postponed it. He is perfectly quiet and comfortable now. Allow me—Miss Rose, will you permit me? Not the slightest fear, I pledge you my honor."

With many more loquacious assurances that they would be agreeably surprised in the aspect of the criminal, the doctor drew the young lady's arm through one of his, and offering his disengaged hand to Mrs. Maylie, led them with much ceremony and stateliness upstairs.

"Now," said the doctor in a whisper, as he softly turned the handle of a bedroom door, "let us hear what you think of him. He has not been shaved very recently, but he doesn't look at all ferocious, notwithstanding. Stop, though—let me see that he is in visiting order first."

Stepping before them he looked into the room, and, motioning them to advance, closed the door when they had entered, and gently drew back the curtains of the bed.

Upon it, instead of the dogged, black-visaged ruffian they had expected to behold, there lay a mere child, worn with pain and exhaustion, and sunk into a deep sleep.

His wounded arm, bound and splintered up, was crossed upon his breast, and his head reclined upon the other, which was half hidden by his long hair as it streamed over the pillow.

The honest gentleman held the curtain in his hand, and looked on for a minute or so in silence. Whilst he was watching the patient thus, the younger lady glided softly past, and seating herself in a chair by the bedside, gathered Oliver's hair from his face, and as she stooped over him her tears fell upon his forehead.

The boy stirred, and smiled in his sleep, as though these marks of pity and compassion had awakened some pleasant dream of a love and affection he had never known. Thus a strain of gentle music, or the rippling of water in a silent place, or the odor of a flower, or the mention of a familiar word, will sometimes call up sudden dim remembrances of scenes that never were in this life, which vanish like a breath, and which some brief memory of a happier existence, long gone by, would seem to have awakened, for no power of the human mind can ever recall them.

When Oliver awoke he told them all his strange history but was often compelled to stop by pain and want of strength.

It was a solemn thing to hear, in the darkened room, the feeble voice of the sick child recounting a weary catalogue of evils and calamities which hard men had brought upon him.

Oliver's pillow was smoothed by women's hands that night, and loveliness and virtue watched him as he slept.

And this, let me tell you, was the end of the poor boy's troubles. It is a very strange thing to have to relate, but the pretty Rose Maylie turned out to be Oliver's aunt—his mother's own sister! From the moment he entered Mrs. Maylie's house his life was as happy as it had been miserable in the past.

From that day forth he saw no more of that
fearful place where the thieves lived, and the
thieves themselves were caught and sent to
prison, and everybody said it served them
right.

JENNY WREN

WALKING into the city one holiday, a great many years ago, a gentleman ran up the steps of a tall house in the neighborhood of St. Mary Axe. The lower windows were those of a counting-house, but the blinds, like those of the entire front of the house, were drawn down.

The gentleman knocked and rang several times before any one came, but at last an old man opened the door. "What were you up to that you did not hear me?" said Mr. Fledgeby irritably.

"I was taking the air at the top of the house, sir," said the old man meekly, "it being a holiday. What might you please to want, sir?"

"Humph! Holiday indeed," grumbled his master, who was a toy merchant amongst other things. He then seated himself in the counting-house and gave the old man—a Jew, and Riah by name—directions as to the various business matters about which he had come to speak, and, as he rose to go, exclaimed—

"By the bye, how *do* you take the air? Do you stick your head out of a chimney-pot?"

"No, sir, I have made a little garden on the leads."

"Let's look at it," said Mr. Fledgeby.

"Sir, I have company there," returned Riah hesitating; "but will you please come up and see them ?"

Mr. Fledgeby nodded, and, passing his master with a bow, the old man led the way up flight after flight of stairs, till they arrived at the house-top. Seated on a carpet, and leaning against a chimney-stack, were two girls bending over books. Some humble creepers were trained around the chimney-pots, and evergreens were placed around the roof, and a few

more books, a basket of gaily colored scraps
and bits of tinsel, and another of common
print stuff, lay near.   One of the girls rose on
seeing that Riah had brought a visitor, but
the other remarked, "I'm the person of the
house downstairs, but I can't get up, whoever
you are, because my back is bad, and my legs
are queer."

"This is my master," said Riah, speaking
to the two girls, "and this," he added, turning
to Mr. Fledgeby, "is Miss Jenny Wren; she
lives in this house, and is a clever little dressmaker for little people.   Her friend Lizzie,"
continued Riah, introducing the second girl.
"They are good girls, both, and as busy as
they are good; in spare moments they come
up here, and take to book learning."

"We are glad to come up here for rest, sir,"
said Lizzie, with a grateful look at the old Jew.
"No one can tell the rest that this place is
to us."

"Humph!" said Mr. Fledgeby, looking round, "Humph!" He was so much surprised that apparently he couldn't get beyond that word, and as he went down again the old chimney-pots in their black cowls seemed to turn round and look after him as if they were saying "Humph" too.

Lizzie, the elder of these two girls, was strong and handsome, but the little Jenny Wren, whom she so loved and protected, was small and deformed, though she had a beautiful little face, and the longest and loveliest golden hair in the world, which fell about her like a cloak of shining curls, as though to hide the poor little mis-shapen figure. Old Riah, as well as Lizzie, was always kind and gentle to Jenny Wren, who called him her godfather. She had a father, who shared her poor little rooms, whom she called her child, for he was a bad, drunken, disreputable old man, and the poor girl had to care for him, and earn money to keep them both.   She suffered a great deal, for the poor little bent back always ached sadly, and was often weary from incessant work, but it was only on rare occasions, when alone or with her friend Lizzie, who often brought her work and sat in Jenny's room, that the brave child ever complained of her hard lot.   Sometimes the two girls, Jenny helping herself along with a crutch, would go and walk about the fashionable streets, in order to note how the grand folks were dressed.   As they walked along, Jenny would tell her friend of the fancies she had when sitting alone at her work.   "I imagine birds till I can hear them sing," she said one day, "and flowers till I can smell them.   And oh! the beautiful children that come to me in the early mornings!   They are quite different to other children, not like me, never cold, or anxious, or tired, or hungry, never any pain; they come in numbers, in long bright slanting rows, all dressed in white, and

with shiny heads.   'Who is this in pain?' they
say, and they sweep around and about me,
take. me up in their arms, and I feel so light,
and all the pain goes.   I know when they are
coming a long way off, by hearing them say,
'Who is this in pain?' and I answer, 'Oh, my
blessed children, it's poor me! have pity on
me, and take me up and then the pain
will go.' "

Lizzie sat stroking and brushing the beautiful hair, whilst the tired little dressmaker
leant against her when they were at home
again, and as she kissed her good-night, a
miserable old man stumbled into the room.
"How's my Jenny Wren, best of children?"
he mumbled, as he shuffled unsteadily towards
her, but Jenny pointed her small finger towards him exclaiming—"Go along with you,
you bad, wicked, old child, you troublesome,
wicked, old thing, *I* know where you have
been, *I* know your tricks and your manners."

The wretched man began to whimper, like a scolded child. "Slave, slave, slave, from morning to night," went on Jenny, still shaking her finger at him, "and all for this; ain't you ashamed of yourself, you disgraceful boy?"

"Yes; my dear, yes," stammered the tipsy old father, tumbling into a corner. Thus was the poor little dolls' dressmaker dragged down day by day by the very hands that should have cared for and held her up; poor, poor little dolls' dressmaker! One day when Jenny was on her way home with Riah, who had accompanied her on one of her expeditions to the West End, they came on a small crowd of people. A tipsy man had been knocked down and badly hurt—"Let us see what it is!" said Jenny, coming swiftly forward on her crutches. The next moment she exclaimed—"Oh, gentlemen—gentlemen, he is my child, he belongs to me, my poor, bad, old child!"

"Your child—belongs to you" repeated the man who was about to lift the helpless figure on to a stretcher, which had been brought for the purpose. "Aye, it's old Dolls—tipsy old Dolls—" cried some one in the crowd, for it was by this name that they knew the old man.

"He's her father, sir," said Riah in a low tone to the doctor, who was now bending over the stretcher.

"So much the worse," answered the doctor, "for the man is dead."

Yes, "Mr. Dolls" was dead, and many were the dresses which the weary fingers of the sorrowful little worker must make in order to pay for his humble funeral, and buy a black frock for herself. Riah sat by her in her poor room, saying a word of comfort now and then, and Lizzie came and went, and did all manner of little things to help her; but often the tears rolled down on to her work. "My poor child," she said to Riah, "my poor old child, and to think I scolded him so."

"You were always a good, brave, patient girl," returned Riah, smiling a little over her quaint fancy about her *child,* "always good and patient, however tired."

And so the poor little "person of the house" was left alone but for the faithful affection of the kind Jew, and her friend Lizzie, but her room grew pretty and comfortable, for she was in great request in her "profession" as she called it, and there was now no one to spend and waste her earnings.

TINY TIM

IT will surprise you all very much to hear
that there was once a man who did not like
Christmas. In fact, he had been heard on
several occasions to use the word *humbug* with
regard to it. His name was Scrooge, and he
was a hard, sour-tempered man of business.
intent only on saving and making money, and
caring nothing for any one. He paid the
poor, hard-working clerk in his office as little
as he could possibly get the work done for,
and lived on as little as possible himself,
alone, in two dismal rooms. He was never
merry or comfortable, or happy, and he hated
other people to be so, and that was the reason why he hated Christmas, because people
will be happy at Christmas, you know, if

they possibly can, and like to have a little money to make themselves and others comfortable.

Well, it was Christmas Eve, a very cold and foggy one, and Mr. Scrooge, having given his poor clerk unwilling permission to spend Christmas Day at home, locked up his office and went home himself in a very bad temper, and with a cold in his head. After having taken some gruel as he sat over a miserable fire in his dismal room, he got into bed, and had some wonderful and disagreeable dreams, to which we will leave him, whilst we see how Tiny Tim, the son of his poor clerk, spent Christmas Day.

The name of this clerk was Bob Crachit. He had a wife and five other children besides Tim, who was a weak and delicate little cripple, and for this reason was dearly loved by his father, and the rest of the family; not but what he was a dear little boy too, gentle and patient

Bob Cratchit and Tiny Tim. (*Page 76*)

and loving, with a sweet face of his own, which no one could help looking at.

Whenever he could spare the time, it was Mr. Crachit's delight to carry his little boy out on his shoulder to see the shops and the people; and to-day he had taken him to church for the first time.

"Whatever has got your precious father, and your brother Tiny Tim!" exclaimed Mrs. Crachit; "here's dinner all ready to be dished up.   I've never known him so late on Christmas Day before."

"Here he is, mother!" cried Belinda, and "Here he is!" cried the other children as Mr. Crachit came in, his long comforter hanging three feet from under his threadbare coat; for cold as it was, the poor clerk had no top-coat. Tiny Tim was perched on his father's shoulder with his little crutch in his hand.

"And how did Tim behave?" asked Mrs. Crachit.

"As good as gold and better," replied the father. "I think, wife, the child gets thoughtful, sitting at home so much. He told me, coming home, that he hoped the people in church who saw he was a cripple, would be pleased to remember on Christmas Day Who it was who made the lame to walk."

"Bless his sweet heart!" said his mother in a trembling voice, and the father's voice trembled too, as he remarked, that "Tiny Tim was growing strong and hearty at last."

Dinner was waiting to be dished up. Mrs. Crachit proudly placed a goose upon the table. Belinda brought in the apple sauce, and Peter the mashed potatoes; the other children set chairs; Tim's, as usual, close to his father's; and Tim was so excited that he rapped the table with his knife, and cried "Hurrah." After the goose came the pudding, with a great smell of steam, like washing-day, as it came

out of the copper; in it came, all a-blaze, with
its sprig of holly in the middle, and was eaten
to the last morsel.   Then apples and oranges
were set upon the table, and a shovelful of
chestnuts on the fire, and Mr. Cratchit served
around some hot sweet stuff out of a jug as
they closed around the fire, and said, "A Merry
Christmas to us all, my dears, God bless us."
"God bless us, every one," echoed Tiny Tim,
and then they drank each other's health, and
Mr. Scrooge's health, and told stories and
sang songs,—Tim, who had a sweet little
voice, singing, very well indeed, a song about
a child who was lost in the snow on Christmas
Day.

Now I told you that Mr. Scrooge had some
disagreeable and wonderful dreams on Christmas Eve, and so he had; and in one of them
he dreamt that a Christmas spirit showed him
his clerk's home; he saw them all gathered

around the fire, and heard them drink his health, and Tiny Tim's song, and he took special note of Tiny Tim himself.

In his dreams that night Scrooge visited all sorts of places and saw all sorts of people, for different spirits came to him and led him about where they would, and presently he was taken again to his poor clerk's home. The mother was doing some needlework, seated by the table; a tear dropped on it now and then, and she said, poor thing, that the work, which was black, hurt her eyes. The children sat, sad and silent, about the room, except Tiny Tim, who was not there. Upstairs the father, with his face hidden in his hands, sat beside a little bed, on which lay a tiny figure, white and still. "My little child, my pretty little child," he sobbed, as the tears fell through his fingers on to the floor. "Tiny Tim died because his father was too poor to give him what was necessary to make him well; *you* kept him poor,"

said the dream-spirit to Mr. Scrooge. The
father kissed the cold, little face on the bed,
and went downstairs where the sprays of holly
still remained about the humble room; and,
taking his hat, went out, with a wistful glance
at the little crutch in the corner as he shut
the door. Mr. Scrooge saw all this, and many
more things as strange and sad—the spirit
took care of that; but, wonderful to relate,
he woke next morning feeling a different man
—feeling as he had never felt in his life before.

"Why, I am as light as a feather, and as
happy as an angel, and as merry as a school-
boy," he said to himself. "A merry Christmas to everybody! A happy New Year to all
the world." And a few minutes later he was
ordering a turkey to be taken round to Tiny
Tim's house, a turkey so large that the man
who took it had to go in a cab.

Next morning poor Bob Crachit crept into

the office a few minutes late, expecting to be roundly abused and scolded for it; he soon found, however, that his master was a very different man to the one who had grudged him his Christmas holiday, for there was Scrooge telling him heartily he was going to raise his salary and asking quite affectionately after Tiny Tim!   "And mind you make up a good fire in your room before you set to work, Bob," he said, as he closed his own door.

Bob could hardly believe his eyes and ears, but it was all true, and more prosperous times came to his family, and happier, for Tiny Tim did not die—not a bit of it.   Mr. Scrooge was a second father to him from that day; he wanted for nothing, and grew up strong and hearty.   Mr. Scrooge loved him, and well he might, for was it not Tiny Tim who had unconsciously, through the Christmas dream-spirit, touched his hard heart, and caused him to be a good and happy man.

LITTLE DAVID COPPERFIELD

LITTLE DAVID COPPERFIELD lived with his mother in a pretty house in the village of Blunderstone in Suffolk. He had never known his father, who died before David could remember anything, and he had neither brothers nor sisters. He was fondly loved by his pretty young mother, and their kind, good servant Peggotty, and David was a very happy little fellow. They had very few friends, and the only relation Mrs. Copperfield talked about was an aunt of David's father, a tall and rather terrible old lady, from all accounts, who had once been to see them when David was quite a tiny baby, and had been so angry to find David was not a little girl, that she had left the house quite offended, and had never been heard of since. One visitor, a tall dark gentleman, David did not like at all, and he was rather inclined to be jealous that his mother should be friendly with the stranger.

One day Peggotty, the servant, asked David if he would like to go with her on a visit to her brother at Yarmouth.

"Is your brother an agreeable man, Peggotty?" he enquired.

"Oh, what an agreeable man he is!" cried Peggotty. "Then there's the sea, and the boats and ships, and the fishermen, and the beach. And 'Am to play with."

Ham was her nephew. David was quite anxious to go when he heard of all these delights; but his mother, what would she do all alone? Peggotty told him his mother was going to pay a visit to some friends, and would be sure to let him go. So all was arranged, and they were to start the next day in the carrier's cart. David was so eager that he wanted to put his hat and coat on the night be-

fore!   But when the time came to say good-by
to his dear mamma, he cried a little, for he
had never left her before.   It was rather a
slow way of traveling, and poor David was
very tired and sleepy when they arrived at
Yarmouth, and found Ham waiting to meet
them.   He was a great strong fellow, six feet
high, and took David on his back and the box
under his arm to carry both to the house.
David was delighted to find that this house was
made of a real big black boat, with a door and
windows cut in the side, and an iron funnel
sticking out of the roof for a chimney.   Inside, it was very cosy and clean, and David
had a tiny bedroom in the stern.   He was
much pleased to find a dear little girl, about
his own age, to play with, and soon discovered
that she and Ham were orphans, children of
Mr. Peggotty's brother and sister, whose fathers had both been drowned at sea, so kind
Mr. Peggotty had taken them to live with him.

An elderly woman, named Mrs. Gummidge, lived with them too, and did the cooking and cleaning, for she was a poor widow and had no home of her own. David thought Mr. Peggotty was very good to take all these people to live with him, and he was quite right, for Mr. Peggotty was only a poor man himself and had to work hard to get a living. David was very happy in this queer house, playing on the beach with Em'ly, as they called the little girl, and he told her all about his happy home; and she told him how her father had been drowned at sea before she came to live with her uncle.

David said he thought Mr. Peggotty must be a very good man.

"Good!" said Em'ly. "If ever I was to be a lady, I'd give him a sky-blue coat with diamond buttons, nankeen trousers, a red velvet waistcoat, a cocked hat, a large gold watch, a silver pipe, and a box of money!"

David was quite sorry to leave these kind
people and his dear little companion, but still
he was glad to think he should get back to
his own dear mamma. When he reached
home, however, he found a great change. His
mother was married to the dark man David did
not like, whose name was Mr. Murdstone, and
he was a stern, hard man, who had no love for
little David, and did not allow his mother to
pet and indulge him as she had done before.
Mr. Murdstone's sister came to live with them,
and as she was even more difficult to please
than her brother, and disliked boys, David's
life was no longer a happy one. He tried to
be good and obedient, for he knew it made
his mother very unhappy to see him punished
and found fault with. He had always had
lessons with his mother, and as she was patient
and gentle, he had enjoyed learning to read,
but now he had a great many very hard lessons
to do, and was so frightened and shy when

Mr. and Miss Murdstone were in the room, that he did not get on at all well, and was continually in disgrace. His only pleasure was to go up into a little room at the top of the house where he had found a number of books that had belonged to his own father, and he would sit and read Robinson Crusoe, and many tales of travels and adventures, and he imagined himself to be the heroes, and went about for days with the center-piece out of an old set of boot-trees, pretending to be a Captain in the British Royal Navy.

But one day he got into sad trouble over his lessons, and Mr. Murdstone was very angry, and took him away from his mother and beat him with a cane. David had never been beaten in his life before, and was so maddened by the pain and by rage that he bit Mr. Murdstone's hand! Now, indeed, he had done something to deserve the punishment, and Mr.

Murdstone, in a fury, beat him savagely, and left him sobbing and crying on the floor, with a dreadful feeling in his heart of how wicked and full of hate he was. David was kept locked up in his room for some days, seeing no one but Miss Murdstone, who brought him his food. At last, one night, he heard his name whispered at the keyhole.

"Is that you, Peggotty?" he asked groping his way to the door.

"Yes, my precious Davy. Be as soft as a mouse or the cat will hear us."

David understood she meant Miss Murdstone, whose room was quite near. "How's Mamma, Peggotty dear? Is she very angry with me?" he whispered. Peggotty was crying softly on her side of the door as David was on his.

"No—not very," she said.

"What is going to be done with me, dear

Peggotty, do you know?" asked poor David, who had been wondering all these long, lonely days.

"School near London—"

"When, Peggotty?"

"To-morrow," answered Peggotty.

"Shan't I see mamma?"

"Yes—morning," she said, and went on to promise David she would always love him, and take the greatest care of his dear mamma, and write to him every week.

"Thank you, thank you, dear Peggotty, and do write and tell Mr. Peggotty, and Em'ly and Ham and Mrs. Gummidge, that I am not so bad as they might suppose, and give them all my love.   Will you, please, Peggotty?"

Peggotty promised, and they both kissed the keyhole most tenderly, and parted.

The next morning David saw his mother, very pale and with red eyes.   He ran to her arms and begged her to forgive him.

"Oh, Davy," she said, "that you should
hurt anyone I love!   I forgive you Davy, but
it grieves me so that you should have such bad
passions in your heart.   Try to be better,
pray to be better."

David was very unhappy that his mother
should think him so wicked, and though she
kissed him and said, "I forgive you, my dear
boy, God bless you," he cried so bitterly when
he was on his way in the carrier's cart, that
his pocket handkerchief had to be spread out
on the horse's back to dry.

After they had gone a little way the cart
stopped, and Peggotty came running up with
a parcel of cakes and a purse for David.
After giving him a good hug, she ran off.

David found three bright shillings in the
purse, and two half-crowns wrapped in paper
on which was written, in his mother's hand—
"For Davy.   With my love."

David shared his cakes with the carrier,

who asked if Peggotty made them, and David told him yes, she did all their cooking.   The carrier looked thoughtful, and then asked David if he would send a message to Peggotty from him.   David agreed, and the message was "Barkis is willing."   While David was waiting for the coach at Yarmouth, he wrote to Peggotty.

"MY DEAR PEGGOTTY,—I have come here safe. Barkis is willing.   My love to Mamma.—Yours affectionately.

"*P.S.*—He says he particularly wanted you to know *Barkis is willing.*"

At Yarmouth he found dinner was ordered for him, and felt very shy at having a table all to himself, and very much alarmed when the waiter told him he had seen a gentleman fall down dead after drinking some of their beer.   David said he would have some water, and was quite grateful to the waiter for drinking the ale that had been ordered for him, for fear the people of the hotel should be offended. The waiter also helped David to eat his dinner, and accepted one of his bright shillings.

After a long, tiring journey by the coach, for there were no trains in those days, David arrived in London and was taken to a school at Blackheath, by one of the masters, Mr. Mell.

When they got to Salem House, as the school was called, David found the holidays were not over, but that he had been sent before the school was opened as a punishment for his wickedness, and was also to wear a placard on his back, on which was written— "Take care of him.   He bites." This made David miserable, and he dreaded the return of the boys. Fortunately for David, the first boy who came back, Tommy Traddles, was not an unkind boy, and seemed to think the placard rather a joke, and showed it to all the boys as they came back, with the remark—

"Look here—here's a game!"

Some of the boys teased David by pretending he was a dog, calling him Towser, and patting and stroking him; but, on the whole, it was not so bad as David had expected. The head boy, too, Steerforth, who was very handsome and some years older than David, said he thought it was "a jolly shame" when he heard all about David's punishment, which consoled the little boy very much. Steerforth promised to take care of him, and David loved him dearly, and thought him a great hero. Steerforth took a great fancy to the pretty, bright-eyed little fellow, and David became a favorite with all the boys, by telling them all he could remember of the tales he had read. He spent all his money the first day on a grand supper in their bedroom (by

Steerforth's advice), and heard many things about the school, and how severe Mr. Creakle, the head master, was. This he found was very true, and the boys were always being caned and punished, especially poor Traddles, who often suffered from his firmly refusing ever to betray any of his schoolfellows.

One day David had a visit from Mr. Peggotty and Ham, who brought two enormous lobsters, a huge crab, and a large canvas bag of shrimps, as they "remembered he was partial to a relish with his meals."

David was proud to introduce his friend Steerforth to these kind simple friends, and told them how good Steerforth was to him, and how he helped him with his work and took care of him, and Steerforth delighted the fishermen with his friendly, pleasant manners.

The "relish" was much appreciated by the boys at supper that night. Only poor Traddles became very ill from eating crab so late.

At last the holidays came, and David went home. The carrier, Barkis, met him at Yarmouth, and was rather gruff, which David soon found out was because he had not yet had any answer to his message. David promised to ask Peggotty for one. When he got home David found he had a little baby brother, and his mother and Peggotty were very much pleased to see him again. They had a very happy afternoon the day he came. Mr. and Miss Murdstone were out, and David sat with his mother and Peggotty, and told them all about his school and Steerforth, and took the little baby in his arms and nursed it lovingly. But when the Murdstones came back David was more unhappy than ever, for they showed plainly they disliked him, and thought him in the way, and scolded him, and would not allow him to touch the baby, or even to sit with Peggotty in the kitchen, so he was not sorry when the time came for him to go back to

school, except for leaving his dear mamma
and the baby.   She kissed him very tenderly
at parting, and held up the baby for him to
see as he drove off in the carrier's cart once
more.

About two months after he had been back
at school he was sent for one day to go into
the parlor.   He hurried in joyfully, for it was
his birthday, and he thought it might be a
hamper from Peggotty—but, alas! no; it was
very sad news Mrs. Creakle had to give him—
his dear mamma had died!   Mrs. Creakle
was very kind and gentle to the desolate little
boy, and the boys, especially Traddles, were
very sorry for him.

David went home the next day, and heard
that the dear baby had died too.   Peggotty
received him with great tenderness, and told
him about his mother's illness and how she
had sent a loving message.

"Tell my dearest boy that his mother, as

she lay here, blessed him not once, but a thousand times," and she had prayed to God to protect and keep her fatherless boy.

Mr. Murdstone did not take any notice of poor little David, nor had Miss Murdstone a word of kindness for the orphan. Peggotty was to leave in a month, and, to their great joy, David was allowed to go with her on a visit to Mr. Peggotty. On their way David found out that the mysterious message he had given to Peggotty meant that Barkis wanted to marry her, and Peggotty had consented. Everyone in Mr. Peggotty's cottage was pleased to see David, and did their best to comfort him. Little Em'ly was at school when he arrived, and he went out to meet her, but when he saw her coming along, her blue eyes bluer, and her bright face prettier than ever, he pretended not to know her, and was passing by, when Em'ly laughed and ran away, so of course he was obliged to run and catch her, and try to kiss her, but she would not let him, saying she was not a baby now. But she was kind to him all the same, and when they spoke about the loss of his dear mother, David saw that her eyes were full of tears.

"Ah," said Mr. Peggotty, running his fingers through her bright curls, "here's another orphan, you see, sir, and here," giving Ham a backhanded knock in the chest, "is another of 'em, though he don't look much like it."

"If I had *you* for a guardian, Mr. Peggotty," said David, "I don't think I should *feel* much like it."

"Well said, Master Davy, bor!" cried Ham, delighted. "Hoorah, well said! no more you wouldn't, bor, bor!" returning Mr. Peggotty's backhander, while little Em'ly got up and kissed her uncle.

During this visit Peggotty was married to Mr. Barkis, and had a nice little house of her own, and David spent the night before he was to return home in a little room in the roof.

"Young or old, Davy dear, so long as I have this house over my head," said Peggotty, "you shall find it as if I expected you here directly every minute. I shall keep it as I used to keep your old little room, my darling, and if you was to go to China, you might think of its being kept just the same all the time you were away."

David felt how good and true a friend she was, and thanked her as well as he could, for they had brought him to the gate of his home, and Peggotty had him clasped in her arms.

Poor little lonely David, with no one near to speak a loving word, or a face to look on his with love or liking, only the two persons who had broken his mother's heart to live with. How utterly wretched and forlorn he felt! He found he was not to go back to school any more, and wandered about sad and solitary, neglected and uncared for. Peggotty's weekly visits were his only comfort. He longed to go to school, however hard an one, to be taught something anyhow, anywhere—but no one took any pains with him, and he had no friends near who could help him.

At last one day, after some weary months had passed, Mr. Murdstone told him he was to go to London and earn his own living. There was a place for him at Murdstone & Grinby's, a firm in the wine trade. His lodging and clothes would be provided for him by his step-father, and he would earn enough for his food and pocket money. The next day David was sent up to London with the manager, dressed in a shabby little white hat, with black crape round it for his mother, a black jacket, and hard, stiff corduroy trousers, a little fellow of ten years old to fight his own battles with the world!

His place, he found, was one of the lowest in the firm of Murdstone & Grinby, with boys of no education and in quite an inferior station to himself—his duties were to wash the bottles, stick on labels, and so on. David was utterly miserable at being degraded in this way, when he thought of his former companions, Steerforth and Traddles, and his hopes of becoming a learned and distinguished man, and shed bitter tears, as he feared he would forget all he had learnt at school. His lodging, one bare little room, was in the house of some people named Micawber, shiftless, careless, good-natured people, who were always in debt and difficulties. David felt great pity for their misfortunes and did what he could to help poor Mrs. Micawber to sell her books and other little things she could spare, to buy food for herself, her husband, and their four children. David was too young and childish to know how to provide properly for himself, and often found he was obliged to live on bread and slices of cold pudding at the end of the week. If he had not been a very innocent-minded, good little boy, he might easily have fallen into bad ways at this time. But God took care of the orphan boy and kept him from harm. The dear little unselfish fellow would not even tell Peggotty how miserable he was, for fear of distressing her.

The troubles of the Micawbers increased more and more, until at last they were obliged to leave London. David was very sad at this, for he had been with them so long that he felt they were his friends, and the prospect of being once more utterly alone, and having to find a lodging with strangers, made him so unhappy that he determined to endure this sort of life no longer. The last Sunday the Micawbers were in town he dined with them. He had bought a spotted horse for their little boy, and a doll for the little girl, and had saved up a shilling for the poor servant girl. After he had seen them off the next morning by the coach, he wrote to Peggotty to ask her if she knew where his aunt, Miss Betsey Trotwood, lived, and to borrow half-a-guinea; for he had resolved to run away from Murdstone and Grinby's, and go to his aunt and tell her his story. He remembered his mother telling him of her visit when he was a baby, and that she fancied Miss Betsey had stroked her hair gently, and this gave him courage to appeal to her. Peggotty wrote, enclosing the half-guinea, and saying she only knew Miss Trotwood lived near Dover, but whether in that place itself, or at Folkestone, Sandgate, or Hythe, she could not tell. Hearing that all these places were close together, David made up his mind to start. As he had received his week's wages in advance, he waited till the following Saturday, thinking it would

not be honest to go before.   He went out to
look for some one to carry his box to the coach
office, and unfortunately employed a wicked
young man who not only ran off with the box,
but robbed him of his half-guinea, leaving
poor David in dire distress.   In despair, he
started off to walk to Dover, and was forced
to sell his waistcoat to buy some bread.   The
first night he found his way to his old school
at Blackheath, and slept on a haystack close
by, feeling some comfort in the thought of the
boys being near.   He knew Steerforth had
left, or he would have tried to see him.

On he trudged the next day and sold his
jacket at Chatham to a dreadful old man, who
kept him waiting all day for the money, which
was only one shilling and fourpence.   He
was afraid to buy anything but bread or to
spend any money on a bed or a shelter for
the night, and was terribly frightened by some
rough tramps, who threw stones at him when

he did not answer to their calls. After six days, he arrived at Dover, ragged, dusty, and half-dead with hunger and fatigue. But here, at first, he could get no tidings of his aunt, and, in despair, was going to try some of the other places Peggotty had mentioned, when the driver of a fly dropped his horse-cloth, and as David was handing it up to him, he saw something kind in the man's face that encouraged him to ask once more if he knew where Miss Trotwood lived.

The man directed him towards some houses on the heights, and thither David toiled. Going into a little shop, he by chance met with Miss Trotwood's maid, who showed him the house, and went in leaving him standing at the gate, a forlorn little creature, without a jacket or waistcoat, his white hat crushed out of shape, his shoes worn out, his shirt and trousers torn and stained, his pretty curly hair tangled, his face and hands sunburnt, and covered with dust.   Lifting his big, wistful eyes to one of the windows above, he saw a pleasant faced gentleman with gray hair, who nodded at him several times, then shook his head and went away.   David was just turning away to think what he should do, when a tall, erect, elderly lady, with a gardening apron on and a knife in her hand, came out of the house, and began to dig up a root in the garden.

"Go away," she said.   "Go away.   No boys here."

But David felt desperate.   Going in softly, he stood beside her, and touched her with his finger, and said timidly, "If you please, ma'am——" and when she looked up, he went on—

"Please, aunt, I am your nephew."

"Oh, Lord!" she exclaimed in astonishment, and sat flat down on the path, staring at him, while he went on—

"I am David Copperfield of Blunderstone, in Suffolk, where you came the night I was born, and saw my dear mamma. I have been very unhappy since she died. I have been slighted and taught nothing, and thrown upon myself, and put to work not fit for me. It made me run away to you. I was robbed at first starting out and have walked all the way, and have never slept in a bed since I began the journey." Here he broke into a passion of crying, and his aunt jumped up and took him into the house, where she opened a cupboard and took out some bottles, pouring some of the contents of each into his mouth, not noticing in her agitation what they were, for David fancied he tasted aniseed water, anchovy sauce, and salad dressing! Then she put him on the sofa and sent the servant to ask "Mr. Dick" to come down. The gentleman whom David had seen at the window came in and was told by Miss Trotwood who the ragged little object on the sofa was, and she finished by saying—

"Now here you see young David Copperfield, and the question is What shall I do with him?"

"Do with him?" answered Mr. Dick. Then, after some consideration, and looking at David, he said, "Why, if I was you, I should wash him!"

Miss Trotwood was quite pleased at this, and a warm bath was got ready at once, after which David was dressed in a shirt and trousers belonging to Mr. Dick (for Janet had burned his rags), rolled up in several shawls, and put on the sofa till dinner-time, where he slept, and woke with the impression that his aunt had come and put his hair off his face, and murmured, "Pretty fellow, poor fellow."

After dinner he had to tell his story all over again to his aunt and Mr. Dick. Miss Trotwood again asked Mr. Dick's advice, and was

delighted when that gentleman suggested that
he should be put to bed.   David knelt down
to say his prayers that night in a pleasant room
facing the sea, and as he lay in the clean,
snow-white bed, he felt so grateful and comforted that he prayed earnestly he might
never be homeless again, and might never forget the homeless.

The next morning his aunt told him she
had written to Mr. Murdstone.   David was
alarmed to think that his step-father knew
where he was, and exclaimed—

"Oh, I don't know what I shall do if I have
to go back to Mr. Murdstone!"

But his aunt said nothing of her intentions,
and David was uncertain what was to become
of him.   He hoped she might befriend him.

At last Mr. and Miss Murdstone arrived.
To Miss Betsey's great indignation, Miss
Murdstone rode a donkey across the green in
front of the house, and stopped at the gate.

Nothing made Miss Trotwood so angry as to see donkeys on that green, and David had already seen several battles between his aunt or Janet and the donkey boys.

After driving away the donkey and the boy who had dared to bring it there, Miss Trotwood received her visitors. David she kept near her, fenced in with a chair.

Mr. Murdstone told Miss Betsey that David was a very bad, stubborn, violent-tempered boy, whom he had tried to improve, but could not succeed; that he had put him in a respectable business from which he had run away. If Miss Trotwood chose to protect and encourage him now, she must do it always, for he had come to fetch him away there and then, and if he was not ready to come, and Miss Trotwood did not wish to give him up to be dealt with exactly as Mr. Murdstone liked, he would cast him off for always, and have no more to do with him.

"Are you ready to go, David?" asked his aunt.

But David answered no, and begged and prayed her for his father's sake to befriend and protect him, for neither Mr. nor Miss Murdstone had ever liked him or been kind to him, and had made his mamma, who always loved him dearly, very unhappy about him, and he had been very miserable.

"Mr. Dick," said Miss Trotwood, "what shall I do with this child?"

Mr. Dick considered. "Have him measured for a suit of clothes directly."

"Mr. Dick," said Miss Trotwood, "your common sense is invaluable."

Then she pulled David towards her, and said to Mr. Murdstone, "You can go when you like. I'll take my chance with the boy. If he's all you say he is I can at least do as much for him as you have done. But I don't believe a word of it."

Then she told Mr. Murdstone what she thought of the way he had treated David and his mother, which did not make that gentleman feel very comfortable, and finished by turning to Miss Murdstone, and saying: "Good-day to you, too, ma'am, and if I ever see you ride a donkey across my green again, as sure as you have a head upon your shoulders, I'll knock your bonnet off and tread upon it!"

This startled Miss Murdstone so much that she went off quite quietly with her brother, while David, overjoyed, threw his arms round his aunt's neck, and kissed and thanked her with great heartiness.

Some clothes were bought for him and marked "Trotwood Copperfield," for his aunt wished to call him by her name.

Now David felt his troubles were over, and he began quite a new life, well cared for and kindly treated.   He was sent to a very nice

school in Canterbury, where his aunt left him
with these words, which David never forgot:

"Trot, be a credit to yourself, to me, and
Mr. Dick, and Heaven be with you.   Never be
mean in anything, never be false, never be
cruel.   Avoid these three vices, Trot, and I
shall always be hopeful of you."

David did his best to show his gratitude to
his dear aunt by studying hard, and trying to
be all she could wish.

When you are older you can read how he
grew up to be a good, clever man, and met
again all his old friends, and made many new
ones.

THE BLIND TOY-MAKER

CALEB PLUMMER and his blind daughter lived alone in a little cracked nutshell of a house. They were toy-makers, and their house, which was so small that it might have been knocked to pieces with a hammer, and carried away in a cart, was stuck like a toad-stool on to the premises of Messrs. Gruff & Tackleton, the Toy Merchants for whom they worked,—the latter of whom was himself both Gruff and Tackleton in one.

I am saying that Caleb and his blind daughter lived here. I should say Caleb did, his daughter lived in an enchanted palace, which her father's love had created for her. She did not know that the ceilings were cracked, the plaster tumbling down, and the woodwork rotten; that everything was old and ugly and poverty-stricken about her, and that her father was a gray-haired stooping old man, and the master for whom they worked a hard and brutal taskmaster;—oh, dear no, she fancied a pretty, cozy, compact little home full of tokens of a kind master's care, a smart, brisk, gallant-looking father, and a handsome and noble-looking Toy Merchant who was an angel of goodness.

This was all Caleb's doing. When his blind daughter was a baby he had determined, in his great love and pity for her, that her deprivation should be turned into a blessing, and her life as happy as he could make it. And she was happy; everything about her she saw with her father's eyes, in the rainbow-colored light with which it was his care and pleasure to invest it. A strange home it was, their living-room was their work-room also, on shelves around it were stored dolls' houses of all sizes and descriptions, dolls' furniture, and dolls themselves of all ranks of life, from the penny plebeian Dutch to the aristocratic wax beauty. There was also a quantity of gay material, out of which the blind girl manufactured dolls' garments. There were piles and rows of Noah's arks, carts and horses, fiddles, drums, and tumblers, and in the midst of it all Bertha sat busily at work, making a doll's frock, whilst Caleb bent over the opposite side of the table painting a doll's house.

"You were out in the rain last night in your beautiful new great-coat," said Bertha.

"Yes, in my beautiful new great-coat," answered Caleb, glancing to where a roughly made garment of sack-cloth was hung up to dry.

"How glad I am you bought it, father."

"And of such a tailor! quite a fashionable tailor, a bright blue cloth, with bright buttons; it's a deal too good a coat for me."

"Too good!" cried the blind girl, stopping to laugh and clap her hands—"as if anything was too good for my handsome father, with his smiling face, and black hair, and his straight figure, as if *any* thing could be too good for my handsome father."

Ah, if poor Bertha could have seen him, with his wasted stooping form and worn face, bending wearily over his work in the squalid little room, I think the sight would have broken her heart.

Caleb began to sing a rollicking song about a sparkling bowl, which made him appear more careworn and poverty-stricken still. "What, you are singing, are you?" growled a gruff voice, as Mr. Tackleton put his head in at the door. "*I* can't afford to sing; I hope you can afford to work too. Hardly time for both, I should say."

"You don't see how the master is winking

at me," whispered Caleb in his daughter's ear
—"such a joke, pretending to scold, you
know."

The blind girl laughed and nodded, and
taking Mr. Tackleton's reluctant hand, kissed
it gently. "What is the idiot doing?" grumbled the Toy Merchant, pulling his hand
away.

"I am thanking you for the little tree, the
beautiful little tree," replied Bertha, bringing
forward a tiny rose-tree in bloom, which, by
an innocent deception, Caleb had made her
believe was her master's gift, though he himself had gone without a meal or two to buy
it.

"Here's Bedlam broke loose. What does
the idiot mean?" snarled Mr. Tackleton; and
giving Caleb some rough orders, he departed
without the politeness of a farewell.

"If you could only have seen him winking

at me all the time, pretending to be so rough to escape thanking," exclaimed Caleb, when the door was shut.

"Always the same," murmured Bertha to herself, "always the same, refusing to be thanked for his thoughtful and generous gifts, always merry and lighthearted in his desire to amuse me when he comes here."

Now a very sad and curious thing had happened. Caleb in his love for Bertha, had so successfully deceived her as to the real character of Mr. Tackleton, making him out everything that was noble and good, and full of thought and care for her, that she had fallen in love, not with her master, but with what she imagined him to be, and was happy in an innocent belief in his affection for her; but one day she was told that he was going to be married, and could not hide from her father the pain and bewilderment she felt at the news.

"Great Heaven!" exclaimed he, when he understood the truth. "Have I deceived you, my poor Bertha, from your cradle, only to break your heart at last"; and the poor old man went on blaming himself until he hardly knew what to do or where to turn for the distress of mind he had caused her, but he felt he must now tell her the truth.

"Bertha, my dear," said Caleb at length, "I have a confession to make to you, there is something on my mind; hear me kindly though I have been cruel to you."

"You cruel to me!" cried Bertha, turning her sightless face towards him.

"Not meaning it, my child! Oh, not meaning it! and I never suspected it till the other day. My poor one, my dear blind daughter, the eyes you trusted have been false to you. The world you live in does not exist as I have painted it; I have concealed things from you which would have given you pain,

I have invented things to please you, and have surrounded you with fancies."

"But living people are not fancies, father, you cannot change them."

"I have done so, my child, God forgive me! I have done so! Bertha, the man who is to be married to-day is in every way unlike what I have described him; he is a hard master to us both, ugly in his looks and in his nature, and hard and heartless as he can be."

"Oh, Heavens! how blind I have been; how could you, father, and I so helpless!" Poor Caleb hung his head. "Answer me, father," said Bertha. "What is my home like?"

"A poor place, Bertha, a very poor and bare place! indeed as little able to keep out wind and weather as my sackcloth coat."

"And the presents that I took such care of, that came at my wish, and were so dearly welcome?" Caleb did not answer. "I see, I understand," said Bertha, "and now I am looking at you, at my kind, loving, compassionate father, tell me what he is like?"

"An old man, my child, thin, bent, grayhaired, worn-out with hard work and sorrow, a weak, foolish, deceitful old man."

The blind girl threw herself on her knees before him, and took his gray head in her arms. "It is my sight, it is my sight restored," she cried. "I have been blind, but now I see, I have never till now truly seen my father. Does he think that there is a gallant, handsome father in this earth that I could love so dearly, cherish so devotedly, as this worn and gray-headed old man. Father, there is not a gray hair on your head that shall be forgotten in my prayers and thanks to Heaven."

"My Bertha!" sobbed Caleb, "and the brisk smart father in the blue coat—he's gone, my child."

"Dearest father, no, he's not gone, nothing

is gone, everything I loved and believed in is here in this worn, old father of mine, and more—oh, so much more, too! I have been happy and contented, but I shall be happier and more contented still, now that I know what you are. I am *not* blind, father, any longer."

POOR JO, THE CROSSING-SWEEPER

JO was a crossing-sweeper; his crossing was in Holborn, and there every day he swept up the mud, and begged for pennies from the people who passed. Poor Jo wasn't at all pleasant to look at. He wasn't pretty and he wasn't clean. His clothes were only a few poor rags that hardly protected him from the cold and the rain. He had never been to school, and he could neither write nor read— could not even spell his own name. He had only one name, Jo, and that served him for Christian and surname too.

Poor Jo! He was ugly and dirty and ignorant; but he knew one thing, that it was wicked to tell a lie, and knowing this, he always told the truth. One other thing poor Jo knew too well, and that was what being hungry means. For little Jo was very poor. He lived in Tom-all-Alones, one of the most horrible places in all London. The road here is thick with mud. The crazy houses are dropping away; two of them, Jo remembered, once fell to pieces. The air one breathes here is full of fever. The people who live in this dreadful den are the poorest of London poor. All miserably clad, all dirty, all very hungry. They know and like Jo, for he is always willing to go on errands for them, and does them many little acts of kindness. Not that they speak of him as Jo.

Oh, dear no! No one in Tom-all-Alones is spoken of by his name, whether it be his surname, or that which his godfathers and godmothers—always supposing that he had any—gave him. The ladies and gentlemen who live in this unfashionable neighborhood have their fashions just as much as the great folks who live in the grand mansions in the West

End.   Here one of the prevailing customs is to give every one a nickname.   Thus it is that if you inquired there for a boy named Jo, you would be asked whether you meant Carrots, or the Colonel, or Gallows, or young Chisel, or Terrier Tip, or Lanky, or the Brick.

Jo was generally called Toughy, although a few superior persons who gave themselves airs and graces, and affected a dignified style of speaking, called him "the tough subject."

Jo used to say he had never had but one friend.

It was one cold winter night, when he was shivering in a doorway near his crossing, that a dark-haired, rough-bearded man turned to look at him, and then came back and began to talk to him.

"Have you a friend, boy?" he asked presently.

"No, never 'ad none."

"Neither have I.   Not one.   Take this,

and Good-night," and so saying, the man who looked very poor and shabby put into Jo's hand the price of a supper and a night's lodging.

Often afterwards the stranger would stop to talk with Jo, and give him money, Jo firmly believed, whenever he had any to give. When he had none, he would merely say, "I am as poor as you are to-day, Jo," and pass on.

One day, Jo was fetched away from his crossing by the beadle, and taken by him to the "Sol's Arms," a public-house in a little court near Chancery Lane, where the Coroner was holding an Inquest—an "Inkwich" Jo called it.

"Did the boy know the deceased?" asked the Coroner.

Indeed Jo had known him; it was his only friend who was dead.

"He was wery good to me, he was," said poor Jo.

The next day they buried the dead man in the churchyard hard by; a churchyard hemmed in by houses on either side, and separated by an iron gate from the wretched court through which one goes to it.

But that night there came a slouching figure through the court to the iron gate. It held the gate with both hands and looked between the bars—stood looking in for a little while, then with an old broom it softly swept the step and made the archway clean. It was poor Jo and as, after one more long look through the bars of the gate, he went away, he softly said to himself, "He was wery good to me, he was."

Now, there happened to be at the Inquest a kind-hearted little man named Snagsby, who was a stationer by trade, and he pitied Jo so much that he gave him half-a-crown.   Half-a-crown was Mr. Snagby's one remedy for all the troubles of this world.

Jo was very sad after the death of his only friend.   The more so as his friend had died in great poverty and misery, with no one near him to care whether he lived or not.

It was a few days after the funeral, while Jo was still living on Mr. Snagsby's half-crown —half a bill Jo called it—that a much bigger slice of good luck fell to his share.   He was standing at his crossing as the day closed in, when a lady, closely veiled and plainly dressed, came up to him.

"Are you the boy Jo who was examined at the Inquest?" she asked.

"That's me," said Jo.

"Come farther up the court, I want to speak to you."

"Wot, about him as was dead?   Did you know him?"

"How dare you ask me if I knew him?"

"No offense, my lady," said Jo humbly.

"Listen and be silent. Show me the place where he lived, then where he died, then where they buried him. Go in front of me, don't look back once, and I'll pay you well."

"I'm fly," said Jo. "But fen larks, you know. Stow hooking it!"

Jo takes her to each of the places she wants to see, and he notices that when he shows her the burying-place she shrinks into a dark corner as if to hide herself while she looks at the spot where the dead man's body rests. Then she draws off her glove, and Jo sees that she has sparkling rings on her fingers. She drops a coin into his hand and is gone. Jo holds the coin to the light and sees to his joy that it is a golden sovereign. He bites it to make sure that it is genuine, and being satisfied that it has successfully stood the test, he puts it under his tongue for safety, and goes off to Tom-all-Alones.

But people in Jo's position in life find it hard to change a sovereign, for who will believe that they can come by it honestly?   So poor little Jo didn't get much of the sovereign for himself, for, as he afterwards told Mr. Snagsby—

"I had to pay five bob down in Tom-all-Alones before they'd square it for to give me change, and then a young man he thieved another five while I was asleep, and a boy he thieved ninepence, and the landlord he stood drains round with a lot more of it."

And so Jo was left alone in the world again, now his friend was dead.   And this poor friend had only two mourners, Jo the crossing-sweeper, and the lady who had come to look at his grave.

Jo mourned for him because he had been his only friend, and the lady mourned for the poor man because she had loved him dearly many years ago when they had both been young together.

As time went on Jo's troubles began in earnest. The police turned him away from his crossing, and wheresoever they met him ordered him "to move on." It was hard, very hard on poor Jo; for he knew no way of getting a living except at his crossing. So he would go back to it as often as he dared, until the police turned him away again. Once a policeman, angry to find that Jo hadn't moved on, seized him by the arm and dragged him down to Mr. Snagsby's.

"What's the matter, constable?" asked Mr. Snagsby.

"This boy's as obstinate a young gonoph as I know: although repeatedly told to, he won't move on."

"I'm always a-moving on," cried Jo. "Oh, my eye, where am I to move to?"

"My instructions don't go to that," the constable answered; "my instructions are that you're to keep moving on. Now the simple question is, sir," turning to Mr. Snagsby, "whether you know him. He says you do."

"Yes, I know something of him, but no harm."

After again cautioning Jo to keep moving on, though to where he still did not say, the constable then moved on himself, leaving Jo at Mr. Snagsby's. There was a little tea-party there that evening, and one of the guests, a very greasy, oily looking man, whom they called Mr. Chadband, and who was a dissenting minister, having by this time eaten and drunk a great deal more than was good for him, determined to improve the occasion by delivering a discourse on Jo. It was very long and very dull to Jo: and in it was this couplet—

"O running stream of sparkling joy,
To be a soaring human boy."

What Jo liked the best was, when the perspiring Chadband had finished, and he was at last allowed to go, Mr. Snagsby followed him to the door and filled his hands with the remains of the little feast they had had upstairs.

And now Jo began to find life harder and rougher than ever. He lost his crossing altogether, and spent day after day in moving on. He grew hungrier and thinner, and at last the foul air of Tom-all-Alones began to have an ill-effect even on him—"the tough subject." His throat grew very dry, his cheeks were burning hot, and his poor little head ached till the pain made him cry. Then he remembered a poor woman he had once done a kindness to, a brickmaker's wife, who had told him she lived at St. Albans, and that a lady there had been very good to her.

"Perhaps she'll be good to me," thought Jo, and he started off to go to St. Albans.

So it came about that one Saturday night, Jo reached that town very tired and very ill. Happily for him the brickmaker's wife met him and took him into her cottage. While he was resting there a lady came in.

The lady sat down by the bed, and asked him very kindly what was the matter.

"I'm a-being froze and then burnt up, and then froze and burnt up again, ever so many times over in an hour. And my head's all sleepy, and all a-going round like, and I'm so dry, and my bones is nothing half so much bones as pain."

"Where are you going?"

"Somewheres," replied Jo, "I'm a-being moved on, I am."

"Well, to-night you must come with me, and I'll make you comfortable." So Jo went with the lady to a great house not far off, and there in a nice warm loft they made a bed for him, and brought him tempting wholesome food. Everyone was very kind to him, even the servants called him "Old Chap," and told him he would soon be well: Jo was really happy, and for a time forgot his pain and fever. But something frightened Jo, and he felt he could not stay there, and he ran out into the cold night air. Where he went he could never remember, for when he next came to his senses he found himself in a hospital. He stayed there for some weeks, and was then discharged, though still weak and ill. He was very thin, and when he drew a breath his chest was very painful. "It draws," said Jo, "as heavy as a cart."

Now, a certain young doctor who was very kind to poor people, was walking through Tom-all-Alones one morning, when he saw a ragged figure coming along, crouching close to the dirty wall. The figure shrank along

with its shapeless clothes hanging to it.   It
was Jo.   The young doctor took pity on Jo.
"Come with me," he said, "and I will find you
a better place than this to stay in," for he saw
that the lad was very, very ill.   So Jo was
taken to a clean little room, and bathed, and
had clean clothes, and good food, and kind
people about him once more, but he was too ill
now, far too ill, for anything to do him any
good.

"Let me lie here quiet," said poor Jo, "and
be so kind anyone as is passin' nigh where I
used to sweep, as to say to Mr. Snagsby as Jo,
wot he knew once, is a-moving on."

One day the young doctor was sitting by
him, when suddenly Jo made a strong effort to
get out of bed.

"Stay, Jo—where now?"

"It's time for me to go to that there burying-
ground."

"What burying-ground, Jo?"

"Where they laid him as was wery good to me, wery good to me, indeed he was.   It's time for me to go down to that there burying-ground, sir, and ask to be put along of him.   I wants to go there and be buried.   He used for to say to me, 'I am as poor to-day as you, Jo,' he says.   I want to tell him that I am as poor as him now, and I want to be along with him."

"By-and-by, Jo, by-and-by."

"Ah, perhaps they wouldn't do it, if I was to go by myself.   But will you promise to have me took there, and laid along with him?"

"I will indeed."

"Thankee, sir.   There's a step there as I used to sweep with my broom.   It's turned very dark, sir, is there any light coming?"

"It's coming fast, Jo."

Then silence for a while.

"Jo, my poor fellow——!"

"I can hear you, sir, in the dark."

"Jo, can you say what I say?"

"I'll say anything you say, sir, for I knows it's good."

"Our Father."

"Our Father—yes, that's very good, sir."

"Which art in Heaven."

"Art in Heaven. Is the light a-coming, sir?"

"It's close at hand. Hallowed be Thy Name."

"Hallowed be Thy——"

The light had come.   Oh yes! the light had come, for Jo was dead.

SMIKE, AND DOTHEBOYS HALL

THE story of poor Smike is told in that wonderful book "Nicholas Nickleby."

Nicholas first met Smike at a school in Yorkshire called Dotheboys Hall, kept by a Mr. Squeers. It was a wretched, miserable place this Dotheboys Hall; Squeers was a hard, wicked man, and Mrs. Squeers was nearly as bad. The first time we hear of Squeers he was in London at "The Saracen's Head," where he occasionally went to bring down new boys, and he was speaking very cruelly to a new little boy, when, just then, a waiter said some one wished to see him. Instantly Squeers changed his manner and pretending he did not know any one was coming said, "My dear child, all people have

141

their trials. This early trial of yours that is fit to make your little heart burst, and your very eyes to come out of your head with crying, what is it? Nothing; less than nothing. You are leaving your friends, but you will have a father in me, my dear, and a mother in Mrs. Squeers. At the delightful village of Dotheboys, near Greta Bridge, in Yorkshire, where youths are boarded, clothed, booked, washed, furnished with pocket money, and provided with all necessaries." But really the boys were half-starved and neglected, and taught nothing, and the most wretched and miserable of all was the poor boy Smike.

Smike had never known a father or a mother. He was beaten and ill-used every day of his unhappy life, and until Nicholas came to Dotheboys Hall, as assistant master, had never known a kind word.

We ought all to be very glad that our schools to-day are not like that terrible place. You can imagine Nicholas's surprise when Mr. Squeers took his class the day after the arrival of the new master.

Obedient to Mr. Squeers' summons, there ranged themselves in front of the schoolmaster's desk half-a-dozen scarecrows, out at knees and elbows, one of whom placed a torn and filthy book beneath his learned eye.

"This is the first class in English spelling and philosophy, Nickleby," said Squeers, beckoning to Nicholas to stand beside him. "We'll get up a Latin one, and hand that over to you. Now, then, where's the first boy?"

"Please, sir, he's cleaning the back parlor window," said the temporary head of the philosophical class.

"So he is, to be sure," rejoined Squeers. "We go upon the practical mode of teaching, Nickleby; the regular education system. C-l-e-a-n, clean, verb active, to make bright, to scour. W-i-n, win, d-e-r, der, winder, a casement. When the boy knows this out of a book he goes and does it. It's just the same principle as the use of the globes. Where's the second boy?"

"Please, sir, he's weeding the garden," replied a small voice.

"To be sure," said Squeers, by no means disconcerted. "So he is, B-o-t, bot, t-i-n, tin, bottin, n-e-y, bottinney, noun substantive a knowledge of plants. When he has learned that bottinney means a knowledge of plants he goes and knows 'em. That's our system, Nickleby. What do you think of it?"

"It's a very useful one, at any rate," answered Nicholas significantly.

"I believe you," rejoined Squeers, not remarking the emphasis of his usher. "Third boy, what's a horse?"

"A beast, sir," replied the boy.

"So it is," said Squeers. "Ain't it, Nickleby?"

"I believe there is no doubt of that, sir," answered Nicholas.

"Of course there isn't," said Squeers. "A horse is a quadruped, and quadruped's Latin for beast, as everybody that's gone through the grammar knows, or else where's the use of having grammars at all?"

"Where, indeed!" said Nicholas abstractedly.

"As you're perfect in that," resumed Squeers, turning to the boy, "go and look after *my* horse, and rub him down well, or I'll rub you down. The rest of the class go and draw water up till somebody tells you to leave off, for it's washing day to-morrow, and they want the coppers filled."

So saying he dismissed the first class to their experiments in practical philosophy, and eyed Nicholas with a look half cunning and half doubtful, as if he were not altogether certain what he might think of him by this time.

"That's the way we do it, Nickleby," he said, after a long pause.

Nicholas shrugged his shoulders in a manner that was scarcely perceptible, and said he saw it was.

"And a very good way it is, too," said Squeers. "Now, just take those fourteen little boys and hear them some reading, because you know you must begin to be useful, and idling about here won't do."

You can quite understand how astonished Nicholas was at all this, for it showed that Mr. Squeers was not only a coarse, common man, but that he could not even spell the most simple words. Nicholas, when school was over, was thinking deeply over the place he had come to, when he all at once encountered the upturned face of Smike, who was on his knees before the stove, picking a few stray cinders from the hearth and planting them on the fire. He had paused to steal a look at Nicholas, and when he saw that he was observed shrunk back as if expecting a blow.

"You need not fear me," said Nicholas, kindly. "Are you cold?"

"N-n-o."

"You are shivering."

"I am not cold," replied Smike, quickly. "I am used to it."

There was such an obvious fear of giving offense in his manner, and he was such a timid, broken-spirited creature, that Nicholas could not help exclaiming, "Poor fellow!"

If he had struck the drudge he would have slunk away without a word. But now he burst into tears.

"Oh dear, oh dear!" he cried, covering his face with his cracked and horny hands. "My heart will break. It will, it will."

"Hush!" said Nicholas, laying his hand upon his shoulder. "Be a man; you are nearly one by years."

"By years!" cried Smike. "Oh dear, dear, how many of them! How many of them since I was a little child, younger than any that are here now! Where are they all?"

"Whom do you speak of?" inquired Nicholas, wishing to rouse the poor half-witted creature to reason. "Tell me."

"My friends," he replied, "myself—my—oh what sufferings mine have been!"

"There is always hope," said Nicholas; he knew not what to say.

"No," rejoined the other; "no, none for me. Do you remember the boy that died here?"

"I was not here, you know," said Nicholas, gently. "But what of him?"

"Why," replied the youth, drawing closer to his questioner's side, "I was with him at night, and when it was all silent he cried no more for friends he wished to come and sit with him, but began to see faces round his bed

that came from home; he said they smiled, and
talked to him; and he died at last lifting his
head to kiss them.   Do you hear?"

"Yes, yes," rejoined Nicholas.

"What faces will smile on me when I die?"
said his companion, shivering.   "Who will
talk to me in those long nights?   They cannot come from home; they would frighten me
if they did, for I don't know what it is, and
shouldn't know them.   Pain and fear, pain
and fear for me, alive or dead.   No hope, no
hope!"   The bell rang for bed, and the boy
subsiding at the sound into his usual listless
state, crept away as if anxious to avoid notice.

After this Nicholas showed what kindness
he could to poor Smike, but his doing so made
things even worse for the unhappy lad.   Mr.
and Mrs. Squeers were more cruel to him
than ever.   After a while, when Nicholas had
made up his mind to leave Dotheboys Hall,
one day he found Smike poring over a tattered

book, with the traces of recent tears still upon his face, trying hard to do his lessons.

The poor soul was vainly endeavoring to master a task which some child of nine years old, possessed of ordinary powers, could have conquered with ease, but which to the addled brain of the crushed boy of nineteen was a sealed and hopeless mystery. Yet there he sat, patiently conning the page again and again, stimulated by no boyish ambition, for he was the common jest and scoff even of the uncouth objects that congregated about him, but inspired by the one eager desire to please his solitary friend.

Nicholas laid his hand upon his shoulder.

"I can't do it," said the dejected creature, looking up with bitter disappointment in every feature. "No, no."

"Do not try," replied Nicholas. The boy shook his head, and, closing the book with a sigh, looking vacantly around, and laid his head upon his arm.   He was weeping.   "Do not," said Nicholas, in an agitated voice; "I cannot bear to see you."

"They are more hard with me than ever," sobbed the boy.

"I know it," rejoined Nicholas.   "They are."

"But for you," said the outcast, "I should die. They would kill me; they would, I know they would."

"You will do better, poor fellow," replied Nicholas, shaking his head mournfully, "when I am gone."

"Gone!" cried the other, looking intently in his face.

"Softly," rejoined Nicholas.   "Yes."

"Are you going?" demanded the boy in an earnest whisper.

"I cannot say," replied Nicholas; "I was speaking more to my own thoughts than to you."

"Tell me," said the boy imploringly. "Oh, do tell me; *will* you go—*will* you?"

"I shall be driven to that at last!" said Nicholas. "The world is before me, after all."

"Tell me," urged Smike, "is the world as bad and dismal as this place?"

"Heaven forbid," replied Nicholas, pursuing the train of his thoughts; "its hardest, coarsest toil were happiness to this."

"Should I ever meet you there?" demanded the boy, speaking with unusual wildness and volubility.

"Yes," replied Nicholas, willing to soothe him.

"No, no!" said the other, clasping him by the hand. "Should I—should I—tell me that again. Say I should be sure to find you."

"You would," replied Nicholas, with the same humane intention, "and I would help

and aid you, and not bring fresh sorrow on you as I have done here."

The boy caught both the young man's hands passionately in his, and hugging them to his breast uttered a few broken sounds, which were unintelligible. Squeers entered at the moment, and he shrunk back into his old corner.

Well, the very next day Smike disappeared. He knew Nicholas was going to leave the school, so the poor lad ran away, hoping some day to meet the only person in the world who had been kind to him.

Mr. Squeers was furious. He hunted high and low, but could not find the runaway. Then Mrs. Squeers set off in the pony and trap to search the country, and a day or two later she found and brought home poor Smike, looking more dead than alive.

The news that Smike had been caught and

brought back in triumph ran like wildfire through the hungry community, and expectation was on tiptoe all the morning. On tiptoe it was destined to remain, however, until the afternoon, when Squeers, having refreshed himself with his dinner, with a countenance of portentous import and a fearful instrument of flagellation, strong, supple, wax-ended and new—in short, purchased that morning expressly for the occasion, asked, in a tremendous voice, "Is every boy here?"

Every boy was there, but every boy was afraid to speak; so Squeers glared along the lines to assure himself, and every eye drooped and every head cowered down as he did so.

"Each boy keep his place," said Squeers, administering his favorite blow to the desk, and regarding with gloomy satisfaction the universal start which it never failed to occasion. "Nickleby, to your desk, sir."

It was remarked by more than one small

observer that there was a very curious and unusual expression on the usher's face, but he
took his seat without opening his lips in reply;
and Squeers, casting a triumphant glance at
his assistant and a look of most comprehensive
despotism on the boys, left the room, and
shortly afterwards returned, dragging Smike
by the collar—or rather by that fragment of
his jacket which was nearest the place where
his collar would have been had he boasted
such a decoration.

In any other place the appearance of the
wretched, jaded, spiritless object would have
occasioned a murmur of compassion and re-
monstrance.   It had some effect even there;
for the lookers-on moved uneasily in their
seats, and a few of the boldest ventured to
steal looks at each other, expressive of indignation and pity.

They were lost on Squeers, however, whose
gaze was fastened on the luckless Smike as he

inquired, according to custom in such cases, whether he had anything to say for himself.

"Nothing, I suppose?" said Squeers, with a diabolical grin.

Smike glanced round, and his eye rested for an instant on Nicholas, as if he had expected him to intercede; but his look was riveted on his desk.

"Have you anything to say?" demanded Squeers again, giving his right arm two or three flourishes to try its power and suppleness.

"Stand a little out of the way, Mrs. Squeers, my dear; I've hardly got room enough."

"Spare me, sir!" cried Smike.

"Oh! that's all, is it?" said Squeers. "Yes, I'll flog you within an inch of your life, and spare you that."

"Ha! ha! ha!" laughed Mrs. Squeers; "that's a good 'un."

"I was driven to do it," said Smike faintly,

and casting another imploring look about him.

"Driven to do it, were you?" said Squeers. "Oh! it wasn't your fault; it was mine, I suppose—eh?"

"A nasty, ungrateful, pig-headed, brutish, obstinate, sneaking dog!" exclaimed Mrs. Squeers, taking Smike's head under her arm, and administering a cuff at every epithet. "What does he mean by that?"

"Stand aside, my dear," replied Squeers. "We'll try and find out."

Mrs. Squeers, being out of breath with her exertions, complied.   Squeers caught the boy firmly in his grip; one desperate cut had fallen on his body—he was wincing from the lash and uttering a scream of pain—it was raised again, and again about to fall—when Nicholas Nickleby, suddenly starting up, cried "Stop!" in a voice that made the rafters ring.

"Who cried stop?" said Squeers, turning savagely round.

"I," said Nicholas, stepping forward. "This must not go on."

"Must not go on!" cried Squeers almost in a shriek.

"No!" thundered Nicholas.

Aghast and stupefied by the boldness of the interference, Squeers released his hold of Smike, and, falling back a pace or two, gazed upon Nicholas with looks that were positively frightful.

"I say must not," repeated Nicholas, nothing daunted; "shall not. I will prevent it."

Squeers continued to gaze upon him; but astonishment had actually, for the moment, bereft him of speech.

"You have disregarded all my quiet interference in the miserable lad's behalf," said Nicholas; "you have returned no answer to the letter in which I begged forgiveness for him, and offered to be responsible that he would remain quietly here. Don't blame me for this

public interference.   You have brought it
upon yourself, not I.''

"Sit down, beggar!'' screamed Squeers, almost beside himself with rage, and seizing
Smike as he spoke.

"Wretch,'' rejoined Nicholas fiercely.
"Touch him at your peril!   I will not stand
by and see it done.   My blood is up, and I
have the strength of ten such men as you.
Look to yourself, for I will not spare you if
you drive me on!''

"Stand back!'' cried Squeers, brandishing
his weapon.

"I have a long series of insults to avenge,''
said Nicholas, flushed with passion; "and my
indignation is aggravated by the dastardly
cruelties practiced on helpless infancy in this
foul den.   Have a care, for the consequences
shall fall heavily upon your own head!''

He had scarcely spoken when Squeers, in a
violent outbreak of wrath, and with a cry like

the howl of a wild beast, spat upon him and struck him a blow across the face with his instrument of torture, which raised up a bar of livid flesh as it was inflicted. Smarting with the agony of the blow, and concentrating into that one moment all his feeling of rage, scorn and indignation, Nicholas sprang upon him, wrested the weapon from his hand, and, pinning him by the throat, beat the ruffian till he roared for mercy.

After beating the schoolmaster, Nicholas packed up a few of his things and started off to find his way back to London; and he had not journeyed far before he was overtaken by Smike, who again had managed to escape. So these two traveled together, with very little money, and meeting with many hardships; but, for all that, they were happier than they had been in that horrid school.

Nicholas always took the greatest care of Smike, and when after a number of adventures he at last got an appointment as clerk in a merchant's office, he took the poor friendless lad to live with him and his mother and sister. These were indeed days of happiness, for they were a happy family, though by no means a rich one.

Unfortunately that wicked Squeers would not leave them alone.   He was resolved to get Smike back again, for Smike was very useful to him in many ways at Dotheboys Hall. So the schoolmaster laid in wait, and one day caught the unfortunate Smike in the streets of London, and carried him off to his lodgings, meaning to take him back to Yorkshire the next day.

But it so happened there was a Yorkshire farmer at Mr. Squeers' lodgings who knew Smike; and he took pity on him, and when all was quiet he went to the room where the lad was locked up, and unlocked the door and told him to run away home as fast as he could.

And you may be quite sure that Smike took his advice. He was soon at home again with the friends he loved so well.

I am sorry to tell you, however, that this happiness did not last long. Poor Smike began to droop, and became more ill day by day and week by week. And he was always haunted with a fearful dread that that awful man Squeers would pounce upon him again and carry him away. The truth was the poor boy was dying.

And now Nicholas began to see that hope was gone, and that upon the partner of his poverty and the sharer of his better fortune the world was closing fast. There was little pain, little uneasiness, but there was no rallying, no effort, no struggle for life. He was worn and wasted to the last degree; his voice had sunk so low that he could scarce be heard to speak. Nature was thoroughly exhausted, and he had laid down to die.

On a fine, mild autumn day, when all was tranquil and at peace, when the soft sweet air crept in at the open window of the quiet room, and not a sound was heard but the gentle rustling of the leaves, Nicholas sat in his old place by the bedside, and knew that the time was nearly come.   So very still it was, that, every now and then, he bent down his ear to listen for the breathing of him who lay asleep, as if to assure himself that life was still there, and that he had not fallen into that deep slumber from which on earth there is no waking.

While he was thus employed, the closed eyes opened, and on the pale face there came a placid smile.

"That's well," said Nicholas.   "The sleep has done you good."

"I have had such pleasant dreams," was the answer.   "Such pleasant, happy dreams!"

"Of what?" said Nicholas.

The dying boy turned towards him, and

putting his arm about his neck made answer, "I shall soon be there!" After a short silence he spoke again. "I am not afraid to die," he said; "I am quite contented. I almost think that if I could rise from this bed quite well I would not wish to do so now. You have so often told me we shall meet again—so very often lately, and now I feel the truth of that so strongly—that I can even bear to part from you."

The trembling voice and tearful eye, and the closer grasp of the arm which accompanied these latter words, showed how they filled the speaker's heart; nor were there wanting indications of how deeply they had touched the heart of him to whom they were addressed.

"You say well," returned Nicholas at length, "and comfort me very much, dear fellow. Let me hear you say you are happy, if you can."

*   *   *   *   *

They embraced and kissed each other on the cheek.

"Now," he murmured, "I am happy."

He fell into a light slumber, and waking, smiled as before; then spoke of beautiful gardens, which he said stretched out before him, and were filled with figures of men, women, and many children, all with light upon their faces; then whispered that it was Eden—and so died.

*   *   *   *   *

One of the strangest things in the poor boy's life was that Nicholas found out some time after that Smike and he were cousins. Isn't it strange how they had been brought together?

Now, before finishing this story, perhaps you would like to know what became of Dotheboys Hall and the unfortunate scholars. Well, Squeers did something more wicked than ever, and was sent to prison, and when the boys heard this they shouted with joy.

Now you must know that the horrible Mrs. Squeers was in the habit of giving all the boys brimstone and treacle, whether they needed it or not.

It was one of the brimstone-and-treacle mornings, and Mrs. Squeers had entered school according to custom with the large bowl and spoon, followed by Miss Squeers and the young Wackford (this was Mr. Squeers' little boy, and a very nasty little boy too), who during his father's absence had taken upon him such minor branches of the executive as kicking the pupils with his nailed boots, pulling the hair of some of the smaller boys, pinching the others, in aggravating places, and rendering himself in various similar ways a great comfort and happiness to his mother.   Their en-

trance, whether by premeditation or a simul-
taneous impulse, was the signal of revolt.
While one detachment rushed to the door and
locked it, and another mounted upon the desks
and forms, the newest (and consequently the
stoutest) boy seized the cane, and confronting
Mrs. Squeers with a stern countenance,
snatched off her cap and beaver bonnet, put it
on his own head, armed himself with the
wooden spoon, and bade her, on pain of death,
go down upon her knees and take a dose directly.   Before that estimable lady could re-
cover herself or offer the slightest retaliation
she was forced into a kneeling posture by a
crowd of shouting tormentors, and compelled
to swallow a spoonful of the odious mixture,
rendered more than usually savory by the
immersion in the bowl of Master Wackford's
head, whose ducking was entrusted to another
rebel.   The success of this first achievement
prompted the malicious crowd, whose faces

were clustered together in every variety of lank and half-starved ugliness, to further acts of outrage. The leader was insisting upon Mrs. Squeers repeating her dose, Master Squeers was undergoing another dip in the treacle, and a violent assault had been commenced on Miss Squeers, when suddenly the door was burst open, and in stepped that same Yorkshire farmer that had helped Smike to run away from Mr. Squeers' lodging in London. The farmer spoke with a peculiar dialect, and I am afraid you would not quite understand it, but this is what he would have said if he had not had a Yorkshire accent:—

"You are nice chaps," said he, looking steadily round. "What's to do here, you young dogs?"

"Squeers is in prison, and we are going to run away!" cried a score of shrill voices. "We won't stop! we won't stop!"

"Well then, don't stop," replied the farmer. "Who wants you to stop? Run away like men, but don't hurt the women."

"Hurrah!" cried the shrill voices more shrilly still.

"Hurrah!" repeated the farmer. "We'll hurrah like men too."

"Hurrah!" cried the voices.

"Another," said the farmer. "Don't be afraid of it. Let's have a good one."

"Hurrah!"

"Now then, let's have one more to end with, and then cut off as quick as you like. Take a good breath now—Squeers is in jail—the school's broke up—it's all over—past and gone—think of that, and let it be a hearty one."

Such a cheer arose as the walls of Dotheboys Hall had never echoed before, and were destined never to respond to again. When the sound had died away the school was empty, and of the busy noisy crowd which had peopled it but five minutes before, not one remained.

LITTLE PAUL DOMBEY

L ITTLE DOMBEY was the son of a rich city
merchant. Ever since his marriage, ten
years before our story commences, Mr. Dombey had ardently desired to have a son. He
was a cold, stern, and pompous man, whose
life and interests were entirely absorbed in his
business, which appeared to him to be the
most important thing in the whole world. It
was not so much that he wanted a son to love,
and to love him, but because he was so desir-
ous of having one to associate with himself
in the business, and make the house once more
Dombey and Son in fact, as it was in name,
that the little boy who was born to him was so
precious, and so eagerly welcomed.

There was a pretty little girl of six years old,
but her father had taken so little notice of her

that it was doubtful if he would have known her had he met her in the street. Of what use was a girl to Dombey and Son? She could not go into the business.

Little Dombey's mother died when he was born, but the event did not greatly disturb Mr. Dombey; and since his son lived, what did it matter to him that his little daughter Florence was breaking her heart in loneliness for the mother who had loved and cherished her!

During the first few months of his life, little Dombey grew and flourished; and as soon as he was old enough to take notice, there was no one he loved so well as his sister Florence. He would laugh and hold out his arms as soon as she came in sight, and the affection of her baby brother comforted the lonely little girl, who was never weary of waiting on and playing with him.

In due time the baby was taken to church, and was given the name of Paul (his father's name). A grand and stately christening it was, followed by a grand and stately feast; and little Paul, when he was brought in to be admired by the company, was declared by his godmother to be "an angel, and the perfect picture of his own papa."

Whether baby Paul caught cold on his christening day or not, no one could tell, but from that time he seemed to waste and pine; his healthy and thriving babyhood had received a check, and as for illnesses, "There never was a blessed dear so put upon," his nurse said. Every tooth had cost him a fit, and as for chicken-pox, whooping-cough, and measles, they followed one upon the other, and to quote Nurse Richards again, "seized and worried him like tiger cats," so that by the time he was five years old, though he had the prettiest, sweetest little face in the world, there was always a patient, wistful look upon it, and he was thin and tiny and delicate. He would be as merry and full of spirits as other children when playing with Florence in their nursery, but he soon got tired, and had such old-fashioned ways of speaking and doing things, that Richards often shook her head sadly over him.

When he sat in his little arm-chair, with his father after dinner, as Mr. Dombey would have him do every day, they were a strange pair—so like, and so unlike each other.

"What is money, papa?" asked Paul on one of these occasions, crossing his tiny arms as well as he could—just as his father's were crossed.

"Why, gold, silver, and copper; you know what it is well enough, Paul," answered his father.

"Oh yes; I mean, what can money do?"

"Anything, everything—almost," replied Mr. Dombey, taking one of his son's wee hands, and beating it softly against his own.

Paul drew his hand gently away. "It didn't save me my mamma, and it can't make me strong and big," said he.

"Why, you *are* strong and big, as big as such little people usually are," returned Mr. Dombey.

"No," replied Paul, sighing; "when Florence was as little as me, she was strong and tall, and did not get tired of playing as I do. I am *so* tired sometimes, papa."

Mr. Dombey's anxiety was aroused, and he summoned his sister, Mrs. Chick, to consult with him over Paul, and the doctor was sent for to examine him.

"The child is hardly so stout as we could wish," said the doctor; "his mind is too big for his body, he thinks too much—let him try sea air—sea air does wonders for children."

So it was arranged that Florence, Paul, and Nurse should go to Brighton, and stay in the house of a lady named Mrs. Pipchin, who kept

a very select boarding-house for children, and
whose management of them was said, in the
best circles, to be truly marvelous. Mr. Dombey himself went down to Brighton every
week, and had the children to stay with him
at his hotel from Saturday to Monday, that he
might judge of the progress made by his son
and heir towards health.

There is no doubt that apart from his im-
portance to the house of Dombey and Son,
little Paul had crept into his father's heart,
cold though it still was towards his daughter,
colder than ever now, for there was in it a sort
of unacknowledged jealousy of the warm love
lavished on her by Paul, which he himself was
unable to win.

Mrs. Pipchin was a marvelously ugly old
lady, with a hook nose and stern cold eyes.
Two other children lived at present under her
charge, a mild blue-eyed little girl who was
known as Miss Pankey, and a Master Bither-

stone, a solemn and sad looking little boy whose parents were in India, and who asked Florence in a depressed voice whether she could give him any idea of the way back to Bengal.

"Well, Master Paul, how do you think you will like me?" said Mrs. Pipchin, seeing the child intently regarding her.

"I don't think I shall like you at all," replied Paul, shaking his head. "I want to go away. I do not like your house."

Paul did not like Mrs. Pipchin, but he would sit in his arm-chair and look at her, just as he had looked at his father at home. Her ugliness seemed to fascinate him.

As the weeks went by little Paul grew more healthy-looking, but he did not seem any stronger, and could not run about out of doors. A little carriage was therefore got for him, in which he could be wheeled down to the beach, where he would pass the greater part of the day. He took a great fancy to a queer crab-faced old man, smelling of sea-weed, who wheeled his carriage, and held long conversations with him; but Florence was the only child-companion whom he ever cared to have with him, though he liked to watch other children playing in the distance. To have Florence by his side, reading or talking to him, whilst the fresh salt wind blew about him, and the little waves rippled up under the wheels of his carriage seemed to perfectly content little Paul.

"I love you, Floy," he said one day to her; "if you went to India as that boy's sister did, I should die."

Florence laid her head against his pillow, and whispered how much stronger he was growing.

"Oh yes, I know, I am a great deal better," said Paul, "a very great deal better. Listen, Floy; what is it the sea keeps saying?"

"Nothing, dear, it is only the rolling of the waves you hear."

"Yes, but they are always saying something, and always the same thing. What place is over there, Floy?"

She told him there was another country opposite, but Paul said he did not mean that, he meant somewhere much farther away, oh, much farther away—and often he would break off in the midst of their talk to listen to the sea and gaze out towards that country "farther away."

After having lived at Brighton for a year, Paul was certainly much stronger, though still thin and delicate. And on one of his weekly visits, Mr. Dombey observed to Mrs. Pipchin, with pompous condescension, "My son is getting on, Madam, he is really getting on. He is six years of age, and six will be sixteen before we have time to look about us." And then he went on to explain that Paul's weak health having kept him back in his studies, which, considering the great destiny before the heir of Dombey and Son, was much to be regretted, he had made arrangements to place him at the educational establishment of Dr. Blimber, which was close by. Florence was, for the present, to remain under Mrs. Pipchin's care, and see her brother every week.

Dr. Blimber's school was a great hothouse for the forcing of boys' brains;—no matter how backward a boy was, Doctor Blimber could always bring him on, and make a man of him in no time; and Dr. Blimber promised speedily to make a man of Paul.

"Shall you like to be made a man of, my son?" asked Mr. Dombey.

"I'd rather be a child and stay with Floy," answered Paul.

Then a different life began for little Dombey.

Miss Blimber, the doctor's daughter, a

learned lady in spectacles, was his special
tutor, and from morning till night his poor
little brains were forced and crammed, till his
head was heavy and always had a dull ache in
it, and his small legs grew weak again—every
day he looked a little thinner and a little paler,
and became more old-fashioned than ever in
his looks and ways—"old-fashioned" was a
distinguishing title which clung to him.   He
was gentle and polite to every one—always
looking out for small kindnesses which he
might do to any inmate of the house.   Every
one liked "little Dombey," but every one down
to the footman said with the same kind of
tender smile—he was such an old-fashioned
boy.   "The oddest and most old-fashioned
child in the world," Dr. Blimber would say
to his daughter; "but bring him on, Cornelia
—bring him on."

And Cornelia did bring him on; and Florence, seeing how pale and weary the little

fellow looked when he came to see her on Saturdays, and how he could not rest from anxiety about his lessons, would lighten his labors a little, and ease his mind by helping him to prepare his week's work. But one day, when his lessons were over, about a fortnight before the commencement of holidays, little Paul laid his weary and aching head against the knee of a schoolfellow of whom he was very fond, and somehow forgot to lift it up again; and the first thing he noticed when he opened his eyes was that the window was open, his face and hair were wet with water, and that Dr. Blimber and the usher were both standing looking at him.

"Ah, that's well," said Dr. Blimber as Paul opened his eyes, "and how is my little friend now?"

"Oh, quite well, thank you, sir," answered Paul, but when he got up there seemed something the matter with the floor, and the walls were dancing about, and Dr. Blimber's head was twice its natural size. Toots, the school-fellow against whom Paul had been leaning, took him up in his arms, and very kindly helped him to bed, and presently the doctor came and looked at him, and said he was not to do any more lessons for the present.

In a few days Paul was able to get up and creep about the house. He wondered some-times why every one looked at and spoke so very kindly to him, and was more than ever careful to do any little kindnesses he could think of for them; even the rough, ugly dog, Diogenes, who lived in the yard, came in for a share of his attentions.

There was to be a party at Dr. Blimber's on the evening before the boys went home, and Paul wished to remain for this, because Florence was coming, and he wanted her to see how every one was fond of him. He was to go away with her after the party. Paul sat in a corner of the sofa all the evening, and every one was very kind to him indeed, it was quite extraordinary, Paul thought, and he was very happy; he liked to see how pretty Florence was, and how every one admired and wished to dance with her. When the time came for them to take leave, the whole houseful gathered on the steps to say good-by to little Dombey and his sister, Toots even opening the carriage door to say it over again. After resting for a night at Mrs. Pipchin's house, little Paul went home, and was carried straight upstairs to his bed. "Floy, dear," said he to his sister, when he was comfortably settled, "was that papa in the hall when I was carried in?"

"Yes, dear," answered Florence.

"He didn't cry, did he, Floy, and go into his own room when he saw me?" Florence could only shake her head, and hide her face against his, as she kissed him.

"I should not like to think papa cried,"

murmured little Paul, as he went to sleep.
He lay in his bed day after day quite happily
and patiently, content to watch and talk to
Florence. He would tell her his dreams,
and how he always saw the sunlit ripples of a
river rolling, rolling fast in front of him;
sometimes he seemed to be rocking in a little
boat on the water, and its motion lulled him
to rest, and then he would be floating away,
away to that shore farther off, which he could
not see. One day he told Florence that the
water was rippling brighter and faster than
ever, and that he could not see anything else.

"My own boy, cannot you see your poor
father?" said Mr. Dombey, bending over him.

"Oh yes; but don't be so sorry, dear papa,
I am so happy,—good-by, dear papa."
Presently he opened his eyes again, and said,
"Floy, mamma is like you, I can see her.
Come close to me, Floy, and tell them," whis-
pered the dying boy, "that the face of the

picture of Christ on the staircase at school is not divine enough; the light from it is shining on me now, and the water is shining too, and rippling so fast, so fast."—The evening light shone into the room, but little Paul's spirit had gone out on the rippling water, and the Divine Face was shining on him from the farther shore.

THE MARCHIONESS

MR. DICK SWIVELLER had just been engaged as clerk to Mr. Sampson Brass, who was a lawyer, and he found to his amazement that his fellow clerk was no other than Mr. Brass's sister, Miss Sally Brass. Miss Sally was a grim and gaunt personage, and Mr. Swiveller, who was a light-hearted and easy-going individual, found his first morning's work in her society so difficult to get through that when she at last went out and left him alone he sprang off his stool and danced a hornpipe. Presently he heard a knock at the front door, and then there came a rapping of knuckles at the office door.

"Come in," said Dick.

"Oh, please," said a little voice, very low down in the doorway, "will you come and show the lodgings?"

Dick leaned over the table and saw a small slipshod girl in a dirty coarse apron and bib, which left nothing of her visible but her face and feet. She might as well have been dressed in a violin case.

"Why, who are you?" said Dick.

To which the only reply was, "Oh, please, will you come and show the lodgings?"

"I haven't got anything to do with the lodgings," said Dick. "Tell 'em to call again."

"Oh, but please will you come and show the lodgings," returned the child; "Miss Sally said I wasn't to, because people wouldn't believe the attendance was good if they saw how small I was at first."

"This is a queer sort of thing," muttered Dick, rising. "What do you mean to say you are—the cook?"

"Yes; I do plain cooking," replied the child. "I'm housemaid too; I do all the work of the house."

It became evident from mysterious thumping sounds in the passage that the applicant for the lodgings would not wait, so Dick Swiveller showed them, and he saw no more of the small servant that day. But he did not forget her. It troubled his mind very much that she seemed always to remain under ground and never came to the surface unless the lodger rang his bell. She never went out, or came into the office, or had a clean face, or took off the coarse apron, or looked out of any of the windows, or stood at the street door for a breath of air, or had any rest or refreshment whatever. Nobody ever came to see her, nobody ever spoke of her, nobody cared about her.

"Now, I'd give something," said Dick to himself, one day, "I'd give something—if I had it—to know how they treat that child and where they keep her."

The office door was open, and at that moment Dick caught a glimpse of Miss Brass's angular figure flitting down the kitchen stairs. "By Jove," thought he, "she's going to feed the small servant. Now or never!"

First peeping over the handrail and allowing Miss Brass to disappear in the darkness below, he groped his way down, and arrived at the door of a back kitchen immediately after Miss Brass had entered the same, bearing in her hand a cold leg of mutton. It was a very dark, miserable place, very low and very damp; the water was trickling out of a leaking butt, and a most wretched cat was lapping up the drops with the sickly eagerness of starvation. Everything was locked up; the coal cellar, the candy box, the salt box, the meat safe, were all padlocked. There was nothing that a beetle could have lunched upon.

The small servant stood with humility in presence of Miss Sally and hung her head.

"Are you there?" said Miss Sally.

"Yes, ma'am," was the answer in a weak voice.

"Go farther away from the leg of mutton, or you'll be picking it, I know," said Miss Sally. The child withdrew into a corner while Miss Brass took a key from her pocket and opening the safe brought from it a dreary waste of cold potatoes, looking about as eatable as Stonehenge.

"Do you see this?" said Miss Brass, slicing off about two square inches of cold mutton, holding it out on the point of the fork.

The small servant, looked hard enough at it with her hungry eyes to see every shred of it, small as it was, and answered, "Yes."

"Then don't you ever go and say," retorted Miss Sally, "that you hadn't meat here. There, eat it up."

This was soon done. "Now, do you want any more?" said Miss Sally.

The hungry creature answered with a faint "No." They were evidently going through an established form.

Miss Sally put the meat away and locked the safe, and drawing near to the small servant, overlooked her while she finished the potatoes, rapping her now on her hand, now on her head, and now on her back, as if she found it quite impossible to stand so close to her without administering a few knocks. Then comforting herself with a pinch of snuff, Miss Brass ascended the stairs, just as Dick had safely reached the office.

What he had seen troubled Dick Swiveller very much, and he thought often of the poor small servant. He was left alone a great deal in the office in the evening with nothing to do, and he used to play cribbage with a dummy.

After a time he began to think that on those evenings he heard a kind of snorting in the direction of the door, which it occurred to him must come from the small servant, who always had a cold from damp living. Looking intently one night he plainly distinguished an eye gleaming and glistening at the keyhole; and he stole softly to the door and pounced upon her before she was aware of his approach.

"Oh, I didn't mean any harm, indeed," cried the small servant, struggling like a much larger one. "It's so very dull downstairs. Please don't tell upon me, please don't."

"Tell upon you!" said Dick. "Do you mean to say you were looking through the keyhole for company?"

"Yes, upon my word I was," replied the small servant.

Dick considered a little.

"Well, come in," he said at last. "There, sit down, and I'll teach you how to play cribbage."

"Oh! I durstn't do it," rejoined the small

servant; "Miss Sally 'ud kill me if she know'd I come up here."

"Have you got a fire downstairs?" said Dick.

"A very little one," replied the small servant.

"Miss Sally couldn't kill me if she know'd I went down there, so I'll come," said Dick. "Why, how thin you are.   Could you eat any bread and meat?   Yes?   Ah!   I thought so. Did you ever taste beer?"

"I had a sip of it once," said the small servant.

"There's a state of things!" cried Mr. Swiveller.   "She's never tasted it—it can't be tasted in a sip!   Why, how old are you?"

"I don't know."

Mr. Swiveller opened his eyes very wide, and vanished straightway.

Presently he returned with a plate of bread

and beef and a great pot, and followed his little companion into the kitchen.

"There!" said Dick, putting the plate before her. "First of all, clear that off, and then you'll see what next."

The small servant needed no second bidding, and the plate was soon empty.

"Next," said Dick, handing the pot, "take a pull at that. Well, is it good?"

"Oh, isn't it!" said the small servant.

Mr. Swiveller then took a long draught himself and applied himself to teaching her the game, which she soon learned tolerably well.

"Now," said Mr. Swiveller, putting two sixpences into a saucer and trimming the wretched candle, "those are the stakes. If you win, you get 'em all. If I win, I get 'em. To make it seem more real and pleasant, I shall call you the Marchioness. Do you hear?" The small servant nodded. "Then,

Marchioness," said Mr. Swiveller, "fire away!"

The Marchioness, holding her cards very tightly in both hands, considered which to play, and Mr. Swiveller put on the gay and fashionable air which such society required. They played until the striking of ten o'clock reminded Mr. Swiveller that he must go before Mr. Sampson and Miss Sally Brass returned.

"With which object in view, Marchioness," said Mr. Swiveller, gravely, "I shall ask your ladyship's permission to retire from the presence. Marchioness, your health! You will excuse my wearing my hat, but the palace is damp, and the marble floor is—if I may be allowed the expression—sloppy."

As a precaution against this latter inconvenience, Mr. Swiveller had been sitting for some time with his feet on the hob, and now he rose.

Dick Swiveller and the Marchioness. (*Page 196*)

"Marchioness," he said, "I am your friend, and I hope we shall play many more rubbers together in this same saloon. But, Marchioness," added Dick, "it occurs to me to ask whether you are in the constant habit of airing your eye at keyholes?"

"I only wanted," replied the trembling Marchioness, "to know where the key of the safe was hid; that was all. And I wouldn't have taken much if I had found it—only enough to squench my hunger."

"You didn't find it, then?" said Dick. "But of course you didn't, or you'd be plumper. Good night, Marchioness."

Now, after this, strange and sad things happened in Mr. Sampson Brass's office, and Mr. Dick Swiveller left off being his clerk. He was very poor indeed, and he lived in one wretched room, and one night he went home to this room and went to bed and was taken very, very ill.

Tossing to and fro upon his hot, uneasy bed, tormented by a thirst which nothing could appease, dreaming endless, weary dreams, the unfortunate Dick lay wasting inch by inch, until at last he sank into a deep sleep and dreamed no more.

He awoke. With a sensation of most blissful rest, he began to remember something of his sufferings, and to think what a long night it had been, until his attention was attracted by a cough. This made him doubt whether he had locked his door last night. Holding the bed curtains open with one hand, he looked out.

The same room certainly, but with what unbounded astonishment did he see all these bottles and basins and such-like furniture of a sick chamber—all very neat and clean, but all quite different from anything he had left there when he went to bed. The atmosphere filled with a cool smell; the floor newly sprinkled; the—the what? The Marchioness? Yes, playing cribbage with herself at the table.

Mr. Swiveller contemplated these things for a short time and then laid his head upon the pillow again.

"I'm dreaming," he thought. "That's clear."

Not feeling quite satisfied with the explanation, Mr. Swiveller presently raised the bed curtains again. The Marchioness dealt, turned up a knave, and omitted to take the usual advantage; upon which Mr. Swiveller called out as loud as he could, "Two for his heels!"

The Marchioness jumped up quickly and clapped her hands, and then began to laugh and then to cry, declaring that she was "so glad, she didn't know what to do."

"Marchioness," said Mr. Swiveller, thoughtfully, "be pleased to draw nearer. First of all will you have the goodness to inform me where I shall find my voice; and secondly, what has become of my flesh?" The Marchioness only shook her head mournfully and cried again.

"I begin to infer, Marchioness," said Dick, "that I have been ill."

"You just have!" replied the small servant, wiping her eyes. "Dead, all but! Three weeks to-morrow! Three long slow weeks."

"Marchioness," said Mr. Swiveller presently, "how's Sally?"

The small servant screwed her face with an expression of the very uttermost entanglement of slyness, and shook her head.

"Bless you," she said, "I've run away."

"And where do you live, Marchioness?" "Live!" cried the small servant. "Here!"

"Oh!" said Mr. Swiveller.

And with that he lay down flat as suddenly as if he had been shot.

"Tell me," he said, "how was it you thought of coming here?"

"Well, you see," returned the Marchioness, "when you were gone I hadn't any friend at all. But one morning, when I was——"

"Was near a keyhole?" suggested Mr. Swiveller.

"Well, then," said the small servant, nodding, "when I was near the office keyhole—I heard somebody saying that she lived here and that you was took very bad, and wouldn't nobody come and take care of you. Mr. Brass, he says, 'It's no business of mine,' he says; and Miss Sally, she says, 'It's no business of mine.' So I ran away that night, and come here and told 'em you was my brother, and I've been here ever since."

"This poor little Marchioness has been wearing herself to death!" cried Dick.

"No, I haven't," she returned; "not a bit of it. Don't you mind about me.

I'm so glad you're better, Mr. Liverer."

"Liverer, indeed!" said Dick, thoughtfully, "it's well I *am* a Liverer. I strongly suspect I should have died, Marchioness, but for you."

From this opinion Mr. Swiveller never departed. Before he had recovered from his illness he inherited some money, and he bought the poor Marchioness a handsome stock of clothes and put her to school forthwith. And when she was nineteen years old they were married, and they played many hundred thousand games of cribbage together. As she had never known her name, he gave her the name of Sophronia Sphynx. But he called her the Marchioness from first to last.

THE FAT BOY

IT was at a grand military review that the Fat Boy first burst in all his glory upon the happy eyes of Mr. Samuel Pickwick, founder and president of the Pickwick Club. Mr. Pickwick was present in the crowd with his three bosom friends—Mr. Tupman, the dandy, Mr. Winkle, the sportsman, and Mr. Snodgrass, the poet,—and had grown very tired and hot with long standing, dazzled with watching the marching, wheeling, and countermarching of regiment after regiment, and nearly deafened by the roar of cheers, the clash of muskets as the troops presented arms, and the noise of brass and pigskins as all the many military bands struck up together. Mr. Pickwick looked round, missing Mr. Tupman, and the next minute missed his hat, which the wind had just blown off his head. It rolled near one of many carriages drawn up in a good position for seeing the troops, and as Mr. Pickwick stooped to pick it up he was hailed from the carriage in Mr. Tupman's hearty voice.

He looked up.

There was a stout gentleman in the carriage with his hand out ready to shake Mr. Pickwick's. There were three ladies, one middle-aged and rather sharp faced, two young and pretty; there was a young gentleman, there was Mr. Tupman, and on the box, sound asleep, sat the very fattest boy Mr. Pickwick had ever set eyes on. Called to sharply by his master, "Joe—bother that boy, he's gone to sleep again!" he rolled slowly off the box, let down the carriage-steps, and held the carriage door invitingly open for the gentlemen. Mr. Winkle mounted to the box, the fat boy waddled to the same perch and fell fast asleep instantly.

"Joe, Joe!" called Mr. Wardle when the sham fight was over and the sham enemies had gone off to dinner, "time for *us* to feed now, eh, Mr. Pickwick? Bother that boy, he's gone to sleep again. Be good enough to pinch him, sir—in the leg, if you please—nothing else wakes him; thank you. Undo the hamper, Joe." The fat boy, roused by a smart pinch from Mr. Winkle, rolled off the box once again, and began to unpack the hamper. He looked fondly upon the various eatables as he uncovered them and handed them up to his master; he beamed upon cold beef, sighed over salad, pored upon pigeon pie, and hung so fondly over a plump, cold, roast fowl that he seemed wholly unable to part with it, and his master had almost to tear it away from him. When he had lost it, for good and all, he tried to find comfort in a veal patty, with which he mounted the box once more, where he very soon again fell asleep.

"Does he always sleep in this way?" asked Mr. Pickwick, glancing where he sat nodding on the box.

"Sleep!" said the old gentleman, "he's always asleep. Goes on errands fast asleep, and snores as he waits at table."

"How very odd!" said Mr. Pickwick.

"Odd, indeed!" said Mr. Wardle. "I'm proud of that boy; wouldn't part with him on any account; he's a natural curiosity. Here, Joe, Joe, take these things away, and help Tom put in the horses."

The fat boy rose, opened his eyes, swallowed the piece of pie which he had been eating when he fell asleep, and slowly obeyed his master's orders, gloating languidly over the remains of the feast as he removed the plates and deposited them in the hamper. The last Mr. Pickwick's party saw of him on that occasion was a

fat form nodding on the box as the carriage rat-
tled away.

When they next set eyes upon him it was
in the setting of his own home—or, rather,
his master's—the Manor Farm, Dingley Dell.
This was a house with a great kitchen and a
lordly larder.   Here he did very little work
and ate and drank prodigiously.

Mr. Wardle and his old mother and his two
pretty daughters, Isabelle and Emily, were
very good-natured and indulgent, and of Joe
was never asked nor expected anything but
the lightest duties.

One of these was to daily lead old Mrs.
Wardle (who was very deaf) to a certain arbor
in the garden, where she would sit and sun
herself in the morning pleasantness.

First of all he had to fetch from a peg behind the old lady's bedroom door a close, black
satin bonnet, a warm cotton shawl and a thick
stick; and then the old lady, after having put

on the bonnet and shawl at her leisure, would lean one hand on her stick and the other on the fat boy's shoulder, and walk leisurely to the arbor, where the fat boy would leave her to enjoy the fresh air for half an hour. Now, the old lady was very precise and particular, and for three summers there had been no change in this particular form of taking the air, so she was very much scared one morning, during the Pickwick party's visit, to see the fat boy, instead of leaving her in the arbor as usual, look carefully round him and then address her very solemnly, "Missus."

The old lady began to shake. "Well, Joe?" she said, wondering if he meant to rob her of her loose coin, knowing that she was too old and feeble to scream for help. "I'm sure I have been a good mistress to you, Joe. You have never had too much to do, and you have always had enough to eat."

This last appeal went straight to the Fat Boy's heart.

"I knows I has," he replied.

"Then what can you want to do now?" asked the old lady. The Fat Boy came closer.

"I wants to make your flesh creep," he said.

"But why?" asked the old lady, trembling again. The Fat Boy explained. He had seen Miss Rachael—Mrs. Wardle's daughter—in this very arbor with one of Mr. Pickwick's party—Mr. Tracy Tupman, to be exact—kissing her hand.

"And she let him?" cried the old lady. "Miss Rachael—my daughter—she let him?"

The Fat Boy nodded till his cheeks shook like a jelly.

But if the Fat Boy could nod, Miss Rachael Wardle could shake her head, and she not only did this, but declared stoutly that what Joe described had never happened, and that he must have dreamt it all.

This for some time put Joe very much out of favor, and any other page-boy with any other master would certainly have lost his place. With Mr. Wardle, however, nobody could be long in disgrace, and before long the Fat Boy was forgiven.

When Christmas time came then, perhaps, the Fat Boy was at his happiest, for then the biggest fires were kept up, and the richest dishes served in dining-room and kitchen alike, and then even the sometimes cross cook grew good tempered for the sake of the pleasant season.

And when one Christmas brought a wedding with it—the wedding of pretty Miss Isabella Wardle to a Mr. Trundle—then the Fat Boy was glorious to see in a new suit, with an enormous white satin favor.

At the wedding breakfast he stole away

every now and then to a corner, where, like little Jack Horner of happy memory he devoured
Christmas pies, though, unlike Jack Horner he
wasted none of his valuable time in picking the
plums out of them.   On Christmas Eve the
family and the servants played games together
in the kitchen.   A huge bunch of mistletoe
was hung up from the kitchen ceiling by Mr.
Wardle's own hands, and all the women in
the house got kissed underneath it, beginning
with the old lady.   Then the games began.
Blind Man's Buff was the first, and Mr. Pickwick himself was the first to be Blindman;
and after that the Fat Boy came into the kitchen, broad awake for once, carrying a great
dish full of flaming brandy and sputtering
raisins, and when fingers enough had been
burned over snapdragon they sat down by a
great log fire to a good supper and a mighty
bowl of wassail, a rich spiced drink of ale and
cordials in which roasted apples were hissing

and bubbling with a pleasant look and a jolly
sound that made every one who heard and saw
them feel as gay as grigs.

Christmas Day itself brought more guests
to Manor Farm—gay and noisy young men,
who made the Fat Boy's life a burden to him
by disturbing him out of a morning nap with
shells of the oysters they had eaten for lunch
aimed skillfully at his nodding head as he sat
in the chimney corner. After church, however, there was an hour on the ice, when the
whole Manor Farm party went off skating, and
the Fat Boy and Sam, Mr. Pickwick's servant,
had a very fine time together on a slide that
they had made.

By the time Christmastide was over and
done with the passing of Twelfth Night, the
Fat Boy was a still fatter boy, and it was a daily
puzzle to guess how he managed to fasten together the many little buttons of his page's
jacket. March winds, April showers, and

May flowers blustered and fell and blossomed around his Humpty-Dumpty-like figure, and only brought it to a riper roundness; and as for his powers of going to sleep without notice, the advancing year only brought them into greater perfection.

* * * * *

Mr. Pickwick and his party had not seen anything of the jolly owner of Manor Farm and the Fat Boy for some months; indeed, flighty spring had grown into beautiful summer and summer had ripened into rich autumn when they met again.

Mr. Pickwick was in London at the time—was, indeed, calling at his lawyer's house—when his path and the Fat Boy's crossed once more.

There came, while the two gentlemen were talking together, a loud and violent knocking at the door, not an ordinary double knock, but a constant supply of the loudest possible single raps, keeping steadily on as if the person outside had learned how to knock but not how to leave off knocking.

The door was opened, and showed them outside a very fat boy standing upright on the mat with his eyes closed in sleep.

The door being opened, Mr. Wardle pushed his way in and shook hands with Mr. Pickwick and the lawyer—who was *his* lawyer too—while the Fat Boy went to sleep again, as he stood.

Here, standing upright and sleeping soundly and sweetly in the mild October sunshine, we must take our leave of him.

It will be pleasant to think of him as never growing any older.

Never any thinner, always a stout Cupid in buttons with shoulder-straps instead of wings.

Always able to eat heartily and sleep

deeply, heart-free and care-free as a young oyster or a young Dutch cheese. Good by, Joe.

"Bother that boy, he's asleep again."

LITTLE DORRIT OF THE MARSHALSEA

MANY years ago, when people could be put in prison for debt, a poor gentleman, who was unfortunate enough to lose all his money, was brought to the Marshalsea prison. As there seemed no prospect of being able to pay his debts, his wife and their two little children came to live there with him. The elder child was a boy of three; the younger a little girl of two years old, and not long afterwards another little girl was born. The three children played in the courtyard, and were happy on the whole, for they were too young to remember a happier state of things.

But the youngest child, who had never been outside the prison walls, was a thoughtful little creature, and wondered what the outside world could be like. Her great friend, the

turnkey, who was also her godfather, became
very fond of her, and as soon as she could
walk and talk, he bought a little arm-chair and
stood it by his fire at the lodge, and coaxed her
with cheap toys to come and sit with him.   In
return the child loved him dearly, and would
often bring her doll to dress and undress as
she sat in the little arm-chair.   She was still a
very tiny creature when she began to understand that every one did not live locked up
inside high walls with spikes at the top, and
though she and the rest of the family might
pass through the door that the great key
opened, her father could not; and she would
look at him with a wondering pity in her
tender little heart.

One day, she was sitting in the lodge gaz-
ing wistfully up at the sky through the barred
window.   The turnkey, after watching her
some time, said:—

"Thinking of the fields, ain't you?"

"Where are they?" she asked.

"Why, they're—over there, my dear," said the turnkey, waving his key vaguely; "just about there."

"Does anybody open them and shut them? Are they locked?"

"Well," said the turnkey, discomfited, "not in general."

"Are they pretty, Bob?" She called him Bob, because he wished it.

"Lovely.   Full of flowers.   There's butter-cups and there's daisies, and there's"—here he hesitated, not knowing the names of many flowers—"there's dandelions, and all manner of games."

"Is it very pleasant to be there, Bob?"

"Prime," said the turnkey.

"Was father ever there?"

"Hem!" coughed the turnkey.   "O yes, he was there, sometimes."

"Is he sorry not to be there now?"

"N—not particular," said the turnkey.

"Nor any of the people?" she asked, glancing at the listless crowd within. "O are you quite sure and certain, Bob?"

At this point, Bob gave in and changed the subject to hardbake. But after this chat, the turnkey and little Amy would go out on his free Sunday afternoons to some meadows or green lanes, and she would pick grass and flowers to bring home, while he smoked his pipe; and then they would go to some tea-gardens for shrimps and other delicacies, and would come back hand in hand, unless she was very tired and had fallen asleep on his shoulder.

When Amy was only eight years old, her mother died, and the poor father was more helpless and broken-down than ever, and as Fanny was a careless child, and Edward idle, the little one, who had the bravest and truest heart, was inspired by her love and unselfishness to be the little mother of the forlorn family, and struggled to get some little education for herself and her brother and sister.   She went as often as she could to an evening-school outside, and managed to get her brother and sister sent to a day-school at intervals, during three or four years.   At thirteen, she could read and keep accounts.   Once, amongst the debtors, a dancing-master came in, and as Fanny had a great desire to learn dancing, little Amy went timidly to the new prisoner, with a bag in her hand, and said—

"If you please, I was born here, sir."

"Oh!   You are the young lady, are you?" said he, looking at the little figure.

"Yes, sir."

"And what can I do for you?"

"Nothing for me, sir, thank you," anxiously undrawing the strings of the little bag; "but if, while you stay here, you could be so kind as to teach my sister cheap."

"My child, I'll teach her for nothing," said the dancing-master, shutting up the bag.

Fanny was a very apt pupil, and the good-natured dancing-master was so pleased with her progress that he went on giving her lessons after his release, which was not for ten weeks, and Amy was so emboldened with the success of her attempt, that when a milliner came in, she went to her on her own behalf, for she had a great desire to learn to do needlework, and begged her to teach her.

"I am afraid you are so weak, you see," the milliner objected.

"I don't think I am weak, ma'am."

"And you are so very, very little, you see," the milliner still objected.

"Yes, I am afraid I am very little indeed," returned the child, and began to sob, so that the milliner was touched, and took her in hand with good will, and found her the most patient and earnest of pupils, and made her a clever workwoman.

But although the father was not too proud to accept "testimonials," in the shape of money and other presents, from the other debtors who pitied the poor gentleman who seemed doomed to pass his life there in that dismal abode, he could not bear the idea that his children should work for their living, so they had to keep it all secret. Fanny became a dancer, and lived with a poor old uncle, who played the clarionet at the small theater where Fanny was engaged. Amy, or Little Dorrit as she was generally called, her father's name being Dorrit, earned small sums by going out to do needlework. She was most anxious to get her brother away from the prison and the bad companions he met with there, and helped by her old friend Bob, she got him into a great many situations. But alas! he was an idle, careless fellow, and always came back to be a burden and care to his poor little sister. At last by dint of pinching and screwing, she saved up enough to send him out to Canada.

"God bless you, dear Tip" (he had been christened Edward, but it had gradually been shortened to Tip), "don't be too proud to come and see us when you have made your fortune," she said.

But Tip only went as far as Liverpool and walked back, being a month on the road, and appeared once more before his poor little second mother in rags, and with no shoes.

In the end, after another trial, Tip returned, telling Amy that this time he had come back in a new way, as "one of the regulars."

"Oh! Don't say you are a prisoner, Tip. Don't, don't!"

But he was—and Amy nearly broke her heart. She implored him not to let her

father know, as it would kill him, and as
Fanny and their uncle joined in her entreaties,
he agreed. So with all these cares and wor-
ries, struggling bravely on, Little Dorrit
passed the first twenty-two years of her life.
Then the son of a lady, Mrs. Clennam, to
whose house Amy went to do needlework, was
interested in the pale, patient little creature,
and learning her history resolved to do his
best to try and get her father released, and to
help them all.

One day when he was walking home with
Little Dorrit to try and find out the names of
some of the people her father owed money to,
a voice was heard calling, "Little mother, little
mother," and a strange figure came bouncing
up to them and fell down, scattering her
basketful of potatoes on the ground. "Oh
Maggie," said Little Dorrit, "what a clumsy
child you are!"

She was about eight-and-twenty, with large

bones, large features, large hands and feet, large eyes and no hair.   Little Dorrit told Mr. Clennam that Maggie was the grand-daughter of her old nurse, who had been dead a long time, and that her grandmother had been very unkind to her and beat her.

"When Maggie was ten years old, she had a fever, and she has never grown older since."

"Ten years old," said Maggie.   "But what a nice hospital!   So comfortable, wasn't it?   Such a Ev'nly place!   Such beds there is there!   Such lemonades!   Such oranges! Such delicious broth and wine!   Such Chicking!   Oh, AIN'T it a delightful place to stop at!"

"Then when she came out, her grandmother did not know what to do with her, and was very unkind.   But after some time, Maggie tried to improve, and was very attentive and industrious, and now she can earn her own living entirely, sir!"

Little Dorrit did not say who had taken pains to teach and encourage the poor half-witted creature, but Mr. Clennam guessed from the name little mother, and the fondness of the poor creature for Amy.

One cold, wet evening, Little Dorrit and Maggie went to Mr. Clennam's house to thank him for having freed Edward from the prison, and on coming out found it was too late to get home, as the gate was locked. They tried to get in at Maggie's lodgings, but though they knocked twice, the people were asleep. As Little Dorrit did not wish to disturb them, they wandered about all night; sometimes sitting at the gate of the prison, Maggie shivering and whimpering.

"It will soon be over, dear," said patient Amy.

"Oh, it's all very well for you, mother," said Maggie, "but I'm a poor thing, only ten years old."

Thanks to Mr. Clennam, a great change took place in the fortunes of the family, and not long after this wretched night, he came to tell Mr. Dorrit that he was the owner of a large property, and so they became very rich.

But little Dorrit never forgot, as, sad to say, the rest of the family did, the friends who had been kind to them in their poverty; and when, in his turn, through no fault of his own, Mr. Clennam became a prisoner in the Marshalsea, Little Dorrit came to comfort and console him, and after a while she became his wife, and they lived happy ever after.

LITTLE NELL AND HER GRANDFATHER

THE house was one of those receptacles for old and curious things, which seem to crouch in odd corners of London town; and in the old, dark, murky rooms, there lived together alone an old man and a child—his grandchild, little Nell. Solitary and monotonous as was her life, the innocent and cheerful spirit of the child found happiness in all things, and through the dim rooms of the old curiosity shop little Nell went singing, moving with gay and lightsome step.

But gradually over the old man, to whom she was so tenderly attached, there stole a sad change. He became thoughtful, dejected, and wretched. He had no sleep nor rest but that which he took by day in his easy chair; for every night, and all night long, he was

away from home.   To the child it seemed
that her grandfather's love for her increased,
even with the hidden grief by which she saw
him struck down.   And to see him sorrowful,
and not to know the cause of his sorrow; to
see him growing pale and weak under his
agony of mind; so weighed upon her gentle
spirit, that at times she felt as though her
heart must break.

At last the time came when the old man's
feeble frame could bear up no longer against
his hidden care.   A raging fever seized him,
and as he lay delirious or insensible through
many weeks, Nell learned that the house
which sheltered them was theirs no longer;
that in the future they would be very poor;
that they would scarcely have bread to eat.

At length the old man began to mend, but
his mind was weakened.

He would sit for hours together, with Nell's
small hand in his, playing with the fingers,

and sometimes stopping to smooth her hair or kiss her brow; and when he saw that tears were glistening in her eyes he would look amazed. As the time drew near when they must leave the house, he made no reference to the necessity of finding other shelter. An indistinct idea he had, that the child was desolate, and in need of help; though he seemed unable to contemplate their real position more distinctly. But a change came upon him one evening, as he and Nell sat quietly together.

"Let us speak softly, Nell," he said. "Hush! for if they knew our purpose they would say that I was mad, and take thee from me. We will not stop here another day. We will travel afoot through the fields and woods, and trust ourselves to God in the places where He dwells. To-morrow morning, dear, we'll turn our faces from this scene of sorrow, and be as free and happy as the birds."

The child's heart beat high with hope and confidence. She had no thought of hunger, or cold, or thirst, or suffering. To her it seemed that they might beg their way from door to door in happiness, so that they were together.

When the day began to glimmer they stole out of the house, and passing into the street stood still.

"Which way?" asked the child.

The old man looked irresolutely and helplessly at her, and shook his head. It was plain that she was thenceforth his guide and leader. The child felt it, but had no doubts nor misgivings, and, putting her hand in his, led him away. Forth from the city, while it yet slumbered, went the two poor adventurers, wandering they knew not whither.

They passed through the long, deserted streets, in the glad light of early morning, until these streets dwindled away, and the open country was about them. They walked all day, and slept that night at a small cottage where beds were let to travelers. The sun was setting on the second day of their journey, and they were jaded and worn out with walking, when, following a path which led through a churchyard to the town where they were to spend the night, they fell in with two traveling showmen, exhibitors of a Punch and Judy show, bound for the races at a neighboring town. And with these men they traveled forward on the following day.

They made two long days' journey with their new companions, passing through villages and towns, and meeting upon one occasion with two young people walking upon stilts, who were also going to the races. The men were rough and strange, as it seemed to

little Nell, in their ways, but they were
kindly too; and in the tumult and confusion
of such scenes as she had never known before,
and in the bewildering noise and movements
of the racecourse, where she tried to sell some
little nosegays, Nell would have clung to them
for protection, had she not learned that these
men suspected that she and the old man had
left their home secretly, and that they meant
to take steps to have them sent back and
taken care of. Separation from her grandfather was the greatest evil Nell could dread.
If they should be found (so the child thought),
people would shut him from the light of sun
and sky, saying that he was mad, and never
let her see him more. She seized her oppor-
tunity to evade the watchfulness of the two
men, and hand in hand she and the old man
fled away together.

That night they reached a little village in a
woody hollow. The village schoolmaster, a

good and gentle man, pitying their weariness, and attracted by the child's sweetness and modesty, gave them a lodging for the night; nor would he let them leave him until two days more had passed.

They journeyed on, when the time came that they must wander forth again, by pleasant country lanes; and as they passed, watching the birds that perched and twittered in the branches overhead, or listening to the songs that broke the happy silence, their hearts were tranquil and serene. But by-and-by they came to a long winding road which lengthened out far into the distance, and though they still kept on, it was at a much slower pace, for they were now very weary and fatigued. The afternoon had worn away into a beautiful evening, when they came to a caravan drawn up by the road. It was a smart little house upon wheels, and at the door sat a stout and comfortable lady, taking tea. The tea-things were set out upon a drum, covered with a white napkin. And there, as if at the most convenient table in the world, sat this roving lady, taking her tea and enjoying the prospect. Of this stout lady Nell ventured to ask how far it was to the neighboring town. And the lady, being kind-hearted, and noticing that the tired child could hardly repress a tear at hearing that eight weary miles lay still before them, not only gave them tea, but offered to take them on in the caravan.

Now this lady of the caravan was the owner of a waxwork show, and her name was Mrs. Jarley. And Mrs. Jarley was won, as the poor schoolmaster had been, by Nell's gentle looks and manner. She offered Nell employ-ment in pointing out the figures in the wax-work show to the visitors who came to see it, promising in return both board and lodging for the child and her grandfather, and some small sum of money. This offer Nell was thankful to accept, and for some time her life and that of the poor, vacant, fond old man, passed quietly and almost happily.

But heavier sorrow was yet to come. One night, a holiday night for them, Nell and her grandfather went out to walk. A terrible thunderstorm coming on, they were forced to take refuge in a small public-house; and here some sinister and ill-favored men were playing cards. The old man watched them with increasing interest and excitement, until his whole appearance underwent a complete change. His face was flushed and eager, his teeth set. With a hand that trembled violently, he seized Nell's little purse, and in spite of her entreaties joined in the game, gambling with such a savage thirst for gain that the distressed and frightened child could almost better have borne to see him dead. The night was far advanced before the play

came to an end, and they were forced to remain where they were until the morning.
And in the night the child was wakened from
her troubled sleep to find a figure in the room
—a figure busying its hands about her garments, while its face was turned to her, listening and looking lest she should awake.   It
was her grandfather himself, his white face
pinched and sharpened by the greediness
which made his eyes unnaturally bright,
counting the money of which his hands were
robbing her.

Evening after evening, after that night, the
old man would steal away, not to return until
the night was far spent, demanding, wildly,
money.   And at last there came an hour
when the child overheard him, tempted beyond his feeble powers of resistance, under-
take to find more money, to feed the desperate
passion which had laid its hold upon his
weakness, by robbing Mrs. Jarley.

That night the child took her grandfather by the hand and led him forth. Through the straight streets and narrow outskirts of the town their trembling feet passed quickly; the child sustained by one idea—that they were flying from disgrace and crime, and that her grandfather's preservation must depend solely upon her firmness unaided by one word of advice or any helping hand; the old man following her as though she had been, an angel messenger sent to lead him where she would.

The hardest part of all their wanderings was now before them. They slept in the open air that night, and on the following morning some men offered to take them a long distance on their barge. These men, though they were not unkindly, were very rugged, noisy fellows, and they drank and quarreled fearfully among themselves, to Nell's inexpressible terror. It rained, too, heavily, and she was wet and cold. At last they reached the great city whither the

barge was bound, and here they wandered up
and down, being now penniless and watched
the faces of those who passed, to find among
them a ray of encouragement or hope.   Ill in
body, and sick to death at heart, the child
needed her utmost firmness and resolution
even to creep along.

They laid down that night, and the next
night too, with nothing between them and the
sky; a penny loaf was all they had had that
day, and when the third morning came, it
found the child much weaker, yet she made
no complaint.   The great manufacturing city
hemmed them in on every side, and seemed
to shut out hope.   Faint and spiritless as
they were, its streets were insupportable; and
the child, throughout the remainder of that
hard day, compelled herself to press on, that
they might reach the country.   Evening was
drawing on; they were dragging themselves
through the last street, and she felt that the

time was close at hand when her enfeebled powers would bear no more. Seeing a traveler on foot before them, and animated with a ray of hope, she shot on before her grandfather, and began in a few faint words to implore the stranger's help. He turned his head, the child clapped her hands together, uttered a wild shriek, and fell senseless at his feet. It was the village schoolmaster who had been so kind to them before.

And now Nell's weary wanderings were nearly over. The good man took her in his arms and carried her quickly to a little inn hard by, where she was tenderly put to bed, and where a doctor arrived with all speed. The schoolmaster, as it appeared, was on his way to a new home. And when the child had recovered somewhat from her exhaustion, it was arranged that she and her grandfather should accompany him to the village whither he was bound, and that he should endeavor to find them some humble occupation by which they could subsist.

It was a secluded village, lying among the quiet country scenes Nell loved. And here, her grandfather being tranquil and at rest, a great peace fell upon the spirit of the child. Often she would steal into the church, and sitting down among the quiet figures carved upon the tombs, would think of the summer days and the bright spring time that would come; of the rays of sun that would fall in, aslant those sleeping forms; of the songs of birds, and the sweet air that would steal in. What if the spot awakened thoughts of death? It would be no pain to sleep amid such sights and sounds as these. For the time was drawing nearer every day when Nell was to rest indeed. She never murmured or complained, but faded like a light upon a summer's evening and died. Day after day and all day long, the old man, broken-hearted and with no love or care for anything in life, would sit beside her grave with her straw hat and the little basket she had been used to carry, waiting till she should come to him again. At last they found him lying dead upon the stone. And in the church where they had often prayed and mused and lingered, hand in hand, the child and the old man slept together.

THE END

The Newbery Classics